*"M... ...
pointing at M...*

Yes, he certainly is, Christa thought. *With a capital* M.

"Man," Robin repeated, this time more insistently.

"I think she wants you to pick her up," Christa prompted. She wondered how he would react. He seemed obviously torn between gruffly dismissing the little girl and giving in to what Christa guessed was a real desire to hold the child.

Robin stamped a tiny, sneakered foot on the concrete. *"Man."*

"Demanding little female, isn't she?" he commented. Before he could reason himself out of it, he bent down to the girl's level and picked her up.

Christa held her breath as she watched them together. They belonged, she thought. Two halves of a puzzle. A man without a child and a child without a father.

It was almost as if they were made for each other. All three of them...

Dear Reader,

From classic love stories to romantic comedies to emotional heart tuggers, Silhouette Romance offers six irresistible novels every month by some of your favorite authors—and some sure to become favorites. Just look at the lineup this month:

In *Most Eligible Dad,* book 2 of Karen Rose Smith's wonderful miniseries THE BEST MEN, a confirmed bachelor becomes a FABULOUS FATHER when he discovers he's a daddy.

A single mother and her precious BUNDLE OF JOY teach an unsmiling man how to love again in *The Man Who Would Be Daddy* by bestselling author Marie Ferrarella.

I Do? I Don't? is the very question a bride-to-be asks herself when a sexy rebel from her past arrives just in time to stop her wedding in Christine Scott's delightful novel.

Marriage? A very happily *un*married police officer finally says "I do" in Gayle Kaye's touching tale *Bachelor Cop.*

In *Family of Three* by Julianna Morris, a man and a woman have to share the same house—with separate bedrooms, of course....

Debut author Leanna Wilson knows no woman can resist a *Strong, Silent Cowboy*—and you won't be able to, either!

I'd love to know what you think of the Romance line. Are there any special kinds of stories you'd like to see more of, less of? Your thoughts are very important to me—after all, these books are for you!

Sincerely,

Melissa Senate,
Senior Editor

Please address questions and book requests to:
Silhouette Reader Service
U.S.: 3010 Walden Ave., P.O. Box 1325, Buffalo, NY 14269
Canadian: P.O. Box 609, Fort Erie, Ont. L2A 5X3

Marie Ferrarella

THE MAN WHO WOULD BE DADDY

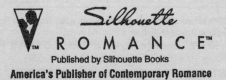

Silhouette
ROMANCE™
Published by Silhouette Books
America's Publisher of Contemporary Romance

To Daddy,
Who finally got it right after all these years.
I miss you.
Love, Marysia.

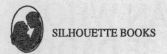 SILHOUETTE BOOKS

ISBN 0-373-19175-8

THE MAN WHO WOULD BE DADDY

This edition published by arrangement with Harlequin Books S.A.

® and TM are trademarks of Harlequin Books S.A., used under license.
Trademarks indicated with ® are registered in the United States Patent
and Trademark Office, the Canadian Trade Marks Office and in other
countries.

Printed in U.S.A.

Books by Marie Ferrarella

Silhouette Romance

The Gift #588
Five-Alarm Affair #613
Heart to Heart #632
Mother for Hire #686
Borrowed Baby #730
Her Special Angel #744
*The Undoing of Justin
  Starbuck* #766
Man Trouble #815
The Taming of the Teen #839
Father Goose #869
Babies on His Mind #920
The Right Man #932
In Her Own Backyard #947
Her Man Friday #959
Aunt Connie's Wedding #984
†*Caution: Baby Ahead* #1007
†*Mother on the Wing* #1026
†*Baby Times Two* #1037
Father in the Making #1078
The Women in Joe Sullivan's Life #1096
‡*Do You Take This Child?* #1145
The Man Who Would Be Daddy #1175

Silhouette Books
Silhouette Christmas Stories 1992
"The Night Santa Claus Returned"

Silhouette Desire
‡*Husband: Optional* #988

Silhouette Special Edition

It Happened One Night #597
A Girl's Best Friend #652
Blessing in Disguise #675
Someone To Talk To #703
World's Greatest Dad #767
Family Matters #832
She Got Her Man #843
Baby in the Middle #892
Husband: Some Assembly Required #931
Brooding Angel #963
‡*Baby's First Christmas* #997

Silhouette Intimate Moments
**Holding Out for a Hero* #496
**Heroes Great and Small* #501
**Christmas Every Day* #538
Callaghan's Way #601
**Caitlin's Guardian Angel* #661
‡*Happy New Year—Baby!* #686

Silhouette Yours Truly
†*The 7lb., 2oz. Valentine*
Let's Get Mommy Married

†Baby's Choice
*Those Sinclairs
‡The Baby of the Month Club

Books by Marie Ferrarella writing as Marie Nicole

Silhouette Romance

Man Undercover #373
Please Stand By #394
Mine by Write #411
Getting Physical #440

Silhouette Desire

Tried and True #112
Buyer Beware #142
Through Laughter and Tears #161
Grand Theft: Heart #182
A Woman of Integrity #197
Country Blue #224
Last Year's Hunk #274
Foxy Lady #315
Chocolate Dreams #346
No Laughing Matter #382

MARIE FERRARELLA

lives in Southern California. She describes herself as the tired
mother of two overenergetic children and the contented wife
of one wonderful man. The RITA-Award-winning author is
thrilled to be following her dream of writing full-time.

Little Robin's Wish List for the Best Birthday Ever:

☺ A visit from Happy Clown to make me and Mommy laugh

☺ Lots and lots of cuddly-wuddly, sooperdoopersize stuffed animals

☺ A shiny new tricycle with ribbons and a basket...

☺ ...and a daddy to put it all together....

☺ Happy Birthday to Me!

Chapter One

She never saw it coming.

One minute, Christa Winslow, newly divorced, newly transplanted former senior accountant of a prestigious Las Vegas–based firm, was just pulling her van into a parking space in front of a convenience store. The next, she was being brutally pulled out of the vehicle and then shoved aside by a tall, wiry man with wild, frightening eyes.

Had she seen him, she would have been prepared and just possibly been able to thwart what he did next. Christa's father and two older brothers, policemen all, had spent long hours seeing to it that she was properly trained to defend herself.

But she hadn't seen him, not until he was beside her, not until he had propelled her away, making her stumble and fall to the ground next to the tread-worn tire of her dusty van. He had caught her off guard and off balance. Trying to break her fall, she twisted her wrist beneath her body at an awkward angle. Christa felt the skin on the palm of her hand rip at the same time that she hit her forehead against the curb.

She had no time to react, no time to be afraid. Her heart was pounding wildly, but only in response to the violence, not in anticipation of what might lie ahead for her.

But it wasn't her the thug wanted. It was her vehicle.

Which made it all the worse.

Turning the key, which was still in the ignition, the carjacker gunned the van's engine as if he were thumbing his nose at Christa in triumph. The next moment, he was peeling out of the lot even as she was scrambling back to her feet.

Oh, God, no. No! Robin!

The horrified protest drummed madly through her brain. A big lump had formed almost instantly on her forehead beneath the fringe of bangs she wore, and the gash on her palm was bleeding now. She could feel the stickiness against her fingers. But all Christa could think of was the van that was speeding away from her. And the precious cargo that was still in it.

"Stop him!" she screamed. "Stop that man. He's stealing my van. My daughter's in it! Somebody, please help me!" The wrenching plea tore out of her throat, rubbing it raw as if every syllable were made out of bits of glass.

The scream shattered the peaceful morning air surrounding the Sylvan Minimall. The handful of people out early in the huge parking lot jerked to attention, looking in Christa's direction. One man came running over to her. But for the most part, the others were immobilized, frozen in place by icy, stunned disbelief. Car-jackings and kidnappings just didn't happen in a quiet place like Bedford.

Except when they did.

"Are you all right?" the man asked Christa.

"No," she cried, watching the van pull away. "No!"

All right? How could she be all right? How could she ever be all right again? Someone had just stolen her child!

Fragments of thoughts collided in her head. She wanted to run after the van and rip the man apart with her bare hands; she wanted to crumple to the ground and cry. She did neither. Instead, she ran into the convenience store to call the police.

Malcolm Evans had gotten a late start this morning.

For all intents and purposes, for him time had stopped moving toward any real goal three years ago on a Sunday afternoon in May. That was when his world had ended in flames.

But he went through the motions of putting one foot in front of the other, and somehow one day followed another, until they knitted themselves into a week, and then a month and then a year.

It made no difference. Nothing changed.

There was a sameness to them all, especially in Southern California. Some days were cooler, some not, but there were no seasons to indicate the passage of the days, no way to differentiate one from another. Malcolm found himself merely existing. Marking time.

The only thing that entered into his life, that made any difference at all, was his sense of responsibility. It was the thin, steely thread that still tethered him to life. He had a place of business. People brought him their cars to repair. So he arrived early, remained late and went home to a place that would never be home again. It would never be more than just a building to him, walls to keep the rest of the world outside.

Usually, he managed to keep his thoughts in an iron Pandora's box, sealed shut. This morning, they had slipped out. The memories. The pain. The guilt.

It had almost swallowed him up, that despair, that loneliness that periodically came out to haunt him ever since Gloria and Sally had been taken from him.

This time, the pain had been almost stronger than he was. But Mr. Mahoney was waiting for him to finish repairs on his pride and joy, a twenty-five-year-old car that defied the odds and continued to run long after it should have become a permanent part of some scrap heap. And God knew if he left Jock on his own all day, the kid would be a basket case before noon.

He had to go in.

So Malcolm had forced himself out of bed, basically proceeding on automatic pilot through his shower and a breakfast a Spartan would have described as meager. He ate for the same reason he did everything else in the past three years: out of an ingrained habit.

Malcolm had just pulled into the northernmost entrance to the minimall, the one closest to his shop, when he heard the woman's screams. The next moment, the van was barreling out of the lot, practically scraping the paint off his car as it passed. The van almost flipped over as it took a turn far more sharply than it should have. Malcolm was so close he could see the wild look on the driver's face.

It violated something within Malcolm to think that crime with its long, dirty fingers, was poking around a city he had always thought of as unblemished. This was the city he had initially chosen to settle in, the city where he had hoped to see his daughter grow to young womanhood. Grow and flourish.

She could do neither now, but somehow it offended her memory to have someone commit a crime in Bedford, especially in broad daylight. Malcolm reacted without thinking and spun around a full 180 degrees to give pursuit.

Driving was second nature to him. It had been ever since he was twelve years old and had finally nagged his uncle into teaching him the fundamental elements of mastering a vehicle. Of course, then it had been a large, unwieldy tractor, but he had swiftly graduated to his cousin's car. And then his mother's tank of a Thunderbird when she had finally been persuaded to give her permission.

By the time Malcolm was sixteen and legally eligible for a learner's permit, he could make a car stand up and beg and do just about anything he wanted it to. Like a centaur in Greek mythology, he was able to meld with his vehicle and become one with it.

For a while, when he was still in high school, he had entertained thoughts of becoming a stunt-car driver. But the lure of the track had been far too great, and he had taken that road.

And abandoned it.

For the past year he'd been driving a LeMans GTO. He had rebuilt the car from the hubcaps on up. It had begun a healing process for Malcolm, and while he hadn't healed, as he worked he had at least found his way out of the darkness. He had pored over every metal scrap, every rod, every cable. Every piece within the car was indelibly marked with his fingerprints.

As he gave chase out of the lot, his car revved to life, performing like a long-sleeping servant eager to please its master.

Keeping an eye out for any passing vehicles, Malcolm commandeered the thoroughfare, wishing for the first time in his life that he owned a car phone. He wanted to call the police and give them his location so that they could cut off the car-jacker before he managed to get away.

Not that he figured the police were really far away. Car chases were uncommon in Bedford. He was certain that by now the squeal of burning rubber had prompted more than one citizen to hurry to his telephone to register a complaint with the police.

With any luck, Malcolm thought, a squad car would shortly be approaching from the other direction to serve as a barricade.

Main Street went from one end of Bedford to the other, serving as a direct link between two freeways. Developments sprouted on both sides of the street, and were lined with carefully crafted stone walls and framed by lush, towering trees that coexisted in landscaping the way they never would have in nature. Right now, a section of the long, winding road was under reconstruction to make it even wider than it was. Detour signs littered the area sporadically, making passage difficult.

The car-jacker was headed straight for the construction area. Obviously not a clear thinker, Malcolm thought. While Freeway 5 was directly on the other side of the reconstruction and closer as an escape route, the smart thing would have been to make a U-turn and head for the 405.

Good thing for the little girl in the van that the guy wasn't smart, Malcolm thought.

The light ahead was turning red. Malcolm knew that wasn't going to be a deterrent to the car-jacker. The van raced through the intersection as a car coming from the right came to a screeching halt, fishtailing and leaving a trail of tire tracks along the asphalt.

Malcolm never hesitated. He pressed down on the accelerator, watching the needle on the speedometer climb to seventy as he rushed to catch up. Seventy was nothing compared to what he had once been accustomed to.

But that had been in another lifetime. When he had had a life. When Gloria and Sally had been a part of it.

Malcolm thought of the woman he'd heard scream. He hadn't even seen her, only heard her voice, heard the anguish in it. It had ripped at his heart, and he knew he had to do something.

Maybe this was why he was still around—to save this woman's baby. Though by all rights, he should have been dead himself twice over.

It seemed to be the only thing that made sense to him.

He watched the rear of the van as the distance between them became shorter. The driver looked as if he was in danger of losing control of the vehicle.

Damn fool.

Up ahead, the road narrowed considerably. Two bulldozers and a crane loomed on both sides of the freshly dug-up road, while orange-jacketed workers littered the area. Main Street's broad lanes were reduced to a single serpentine path.

If he followed the curving path, he would still be behind the van. And he needed to be in front of it to make the driver brake.

Malcolm made his decision.

Hands tightening on the wheel, he plowed through the wooden horse barricade, then sailed over a mound of dirt and broken concrete that hadn't been hauled away yet. For one moment, he was airborne. The next moment, the earth was there to greet him. Malcolm could feel his teeth rattling in his mouth as the LeMans came down hard onto the road. Dirt was flying everywhere.

He was going to have some heavy-duty work on his hands with the car later, he thought vaguely.

As he floored the accelerator, the LeMans seemed to fly forward, directly ahead of the van. He passed it, then, twisting his wheel hard, Malcolm spun around a full 180 degrees, bringing the hood of his car physically into the path of the van.

He saw the horrified look on the car-jacker's face as the distance between the cars dissolved. The next moment, his curses swallowed up by the scream of tires and brakes locking, the man frantically tried to prevent a crash.

On the periphery of his consciousness, Malcolm saw men in the area scrambling to get out of the way of what looked like the inevitable. With the skill of a man who had earned his living and his reputation driving at high speeds for the entertainment of others, Malcolm pulled back, avoiding the impact that had seemed so certain a second ago.

And then came the stern peal of sirens as white cars with blue-and-red dancing lights atop their roofs seemed to materialize from every direction. They converged, surrounding the van and Malcolm's LeMans.

He didn't wait for them. Didn't wait for the inevitable questions to assault his sense of privacy. Jumping out of his car, Malcolm hurried to the van. He didn't give a damn about the driver, who was slumped forward over the wheel. At the last moment, his head had come in contact with the windshield, and while the wheel had prevented him from going through the glass, he'd hit his head and obviously been knocked out.

He could have been dead for all Malcolm cared. That was for the police to handle. Yanking the passenger door open, Malcolm climbed in, scanning the interior for signs of another occupant. A high-pitched wail that somehow managed to rise above the sound of the sirens guided him to the car seat directly behind the driver. And to the unwilling participant in the short-lived joyride.

It was a little girl, hardly more than a toddler. He hadn't expected her to be so young. So much like Sally.

The next second, Malcolm felt someone grab his wrist. The car-jacker had come to. With his other hand, he was reaching for the gun that was shoved far too cavalierly in his waistband.

"Hey, man, what the hell did you think you were doing?" the car-jacker demanded.

The car-jacker had no opportunity for any further questions or threats. A service revolver was trained at his head as the young policeman on the other side of the driver's window loudly ordered him to remove his hand from the butt of his gun.

Losing his nerve, the man instantly raised both hands above his head. A barrage of impotent curses flooded the air as he was unceremoniously yanked from the van by one of Bedford's finest.

"You watch your mouth around the baby," the officer warned.

The baby cried louder.

Memories multiplied and changed, like a kaleidoscope rolling down a hill, bursting through Malcolm's brain. "Hey, it's okay," he said in a soft, low voice as he approached the child.

Wide cornflower blue eyes stared at him as the cries faded into the air as quickly as they had come. The little girl had hair as blond as the rays of the morning sun. Captivated, Malcolm smiled at her as he unbuckled the straps restraining her.

Her eyes, huge with wonder, seemed to look right into him.

"Some joyride, huh?" he murmured as he lifted her from her seat. She was wearing rompers, he thought. And looked to be probably around Sally's age.

Or what Sally's age had been three years ago, he amended silently.

Holding the little girl against his chest, he cupped his hand protectively over the back of her head and carefully retraced his steps out of the van. He murmured softly to the child to keep her from crying again. Bittersweet sensations filled him. It had been so long since he had held a little girl this way, he thought. Much too long.

Suddenly, Malcolm found himself flanked on three sides by policemen, none of whom looked as if he knew exactly what to make of Malcolm's part in this unorthodox chase down Main Street.

"Here, let me take her," one of the policemen said to Malcolm.

He felt the slight nudge of reluctance as he surrendered the child to the younger man. "She looks none the worse for wear," Malcolm observed.

"No, I guess she doesn't," the policeman agreed, his voice thick with emotion.

Only when he held his niece safe in his arms did relief flood Officer Tyler McGuire. News of the car-jacking had crackled over the radio, interrupting a conversation he'd been having with his partner. There'd been instant recognition when the dispatcher recited the van's license-plate number. Instant recognition and instant fear that Tyler had had to hold in check as he sprang into action.

Satisfied that Robin was all right, Tyler raised his eyes to the stranger's face. He didn't know him. "That's in part thanks to you," he replied. "I have no idea who you are, but I'm sure glad you came along when you did. Where did you learn how to drive like that?"

A distant smile quirked Malcolm's lips. "On a farm."

Now that the baby was safe, the adrenaline was slowly wearing off. He was really going to have to do some catching up today, he thought. He'd promised Mahoney the car by two.

Tyler laughed as Robin gurgled at him. "Must have been one hell of a farm," he commented. "If it weren't for you," Tyler told him, sobering, "she might have become just another statistic."

Malcolm didn't want praise or gratitude; he was just happy to set things right. He shrugged away the officer's words as he began heading back to his car. "Just a matter of being in the right place at the right time, that's all."

"Mind following me back?" Tyler called out to him. It was more of an invitation than a question. "My sister is going to want to thank you for this in person."

Malcolm stopped beside his car. "Sister?" What did the policeman's sister have to do with anything?

He nodded. "Christa. The woman whose baby you just saved." Tyler shifted Robin to his other side and thought how good it felt just to hold her. "This is my niece, Robin Winslow."

Malcolm paused and looked into the face of the child he had rescued. He thought of Sally again and felt his heart squeeze a little. "Nice to meet you, Robin Winslow."

Tyler thought he detected a hint of a smile on the man's lips before it faded.

"C'mon back to the minimall," Tyler urged again as he opened the van's passenger door. "Christa's still waiting there." If he knew his sister, she would remain there indefinitely, praying for a miracle. It looked as if this time she'd gotten one.

They all had, he amended, looking at Robin. "By the way, my name's Tyler McGuire."

"Malcolm Evans," Malcolm said after a moment.

Tyler shook his hand. "I am *really* glad to meet you. C'mon, Robin, let's go see Mommy."

"Mommy," Robin affirmed.

Tyler laughed as he hugged her. "I'll drive the van," he told his partner. "Follow me back."

His partner, Elliott, nodded and started up the squad car. The other two cars had gone directly to the police station with their prisoner in custody. The man would be spending the night in a holding cell courtesy of the city, and tomorrow, after charges were pressed, he would find himself with another mailing address.

Not waiting for the policeman to go first, Malcolm turned his LeMans around and headed straight toward the minimall.

It surprised him that the incident could have stirred so many memories within him. It was like someone poking a stick at the embers of a fire that hadn't quite managed to go out.

It was all because he'd held the child, he thought. Holding her had made him remember. And yearn.

And regret.

He blew out a breath, wishing there was some effective way to permanently anesthetize himself so that he didn't feel anything anymore. Feeling nothing was preferable to feeling pain.

He took the yellow light automatically and turned down the street that fed into the minimall. And saw her. Even some distance away, he knew it had to be her, the woman who had screamed. The woman whose child he'd saved. She couldn't have been anyone else. The woman, her hair as blond as her daughter's, was standing on the northernmost curb of the minimall, frantically searching the thoroughfare for some sight of her van.

The way she stood, alert, poised, hopeful, made him think of a portrait of a woman from the old seafaring days. Days when women stood watch upon the widow's walk of a Cape Cod house, looking at the sea for some sign of their husbands' ships on the horizon.

As soon as she caught sight of the van, Malcolm saw a smile break out over her face. Even at a distance, it was nothing short of radiant.

So radiant that he found himself caught up in its brilliance. It made him feel good for the first time in years. It felt like sunshine seeping through the pores after months in the gloomy mist.

Malcolm saw the woman hurrying past his car, reaching the door of the van before it had come to a full stop. As she ran by, he saw the tears streaming down her face, tears that were in direct contradiction to the smile on her face.

"You got her back!" Christa cried.

Disbelief, joy and relief all tangled together in her voice. Her hands trembled as she opened the door and quickly climbed inside. They shook even more as she snapped open the harness that held Robin in place. She was certain that her heart was going to crack through her ribs as it pounded hard in relief.

"Not me," Tyler told her as he got out of the vehicle. "He did." Tyler jerked his thumb at Malcolm's car.

Daughter pressed against her, Christa sobbed her relief into Robin's hair. Then, pulling herself together, she stepped out of the van. With Robin in her arms, Christa turned to look at the man her brother had pointed out, the man whom she had seen tearing out after the carjacker.

The man who had given her back the life she saw flowing away from her only fifteen minutes earlier.

"I have no idea how to thank you," Christa cried. Emotion choked her words away, and she threw her free arm about his neck and hugged him.

Caught in an emotional embrace between the woman and the child in her arms, Malcolm was temporarily at a loss. The last time he'd been standing like this, it had been Gloria and Sally whose embrace he'd shared. Sally with her perpetually sticky fingers, and Gloria, who had smelled like roses. This woman smelled of wildflowers. Memories battered at him, threatening to overwhelm him completely.

They assaulted him even harder as the woman brushed a kiss on his cheek.

He swallowed, separating himself from both of them. "I think that'll do just fine," he told her.

Christa wondered why she saw a hint of longing in his eyes as he looked at Robin before stepping away.

"Glad I could help," he murmured. "Take care of her. Every day is precious."

And then, just like that, he turned and walked away.

Chapter Two

It took a minute before the image of the retreating back registered. He was walking away. The man who had given her back the very meaning of her life was walking away, and she didn't even know his name.

Holding her daughter pressed close to her breast, Christa hurried after Malcolm. Behind her, she heard her brother calling after her.

"Christa, you all right?" Bewilderment tinged his question.

She didn't turn around. Instead, she held Robin a little tighter as she increased her stride. The little girl squirmed and wriggled against her in protest, but after what she'd just been through, there was no way Christa was going to set Robin down. At least, not yet.

"Yes, I'm fine," she answered.

Her Good Samaritan, almost a foot taller than she, had a long stride that took him farther and farther away from her with every step. The only way she could catch up was if she ran. Weighed down, she couldn't, but her eyes never left her target.

Why had he walked away from her just like that, as if he'd only picked up a pencil she'd dropped and returned it to her? Surely the impact of the situation had to have registered. Without even knowing her, he'd risked his life to get her daughter back. Why wouldn't he let her thank him?

Feeling the weight of the huge debt she owed him, that she would always owe him, Christa couldn't allow this moment to pass as if it were nothing.

"Mommy?" Robin whimpered, squirming again.

Christa kissed the top of her daughter's head, but she didn't slow down. "In a minute, honey. Mommy has to see someone."

Her arms were locked tightly around Robin. She wished she could make a haven out of them, a haven that would keep Robin safe forever.

But she was safe now, thanks to him.

If nothing else, Christa needed to know what his name was.

Perspiration dripped into Jock Peritoni's eyes as he looked up from the hot, uncooperative engine he'd been struggling with for the past half hour. The test drive he'd just taken the vehicle on had told him nothing. He didn't have his father's or Malcolm's ear. He couldn't just listen and be able to narrow down a problem.

He'd been only vaguely aware of the squealing tires and the life-and-death race that had taken place in the far end of the minimall. The engine had absorbed all his attention. He'd wanted to fix it before Malcolm arrived at work.

So far, all his efforts had been wasted.

Relief highlighted his grease-streaked face as he saw Malcolm approach. He'd begun to worry that something was wrong and his boss wasn't coming in today. Malcolm was never late.

It was only ten minutes shy of nine in the morning, but Jock already felt himself overwhelmed. Wiping his hands on the back of his permanently stained jeans, the nineteen-year-old noticed the woman with the little girl in her arms. It looked as if she was hurrying to catch up to his boss, but Malcolm seemed completely oblivious to the fact that he was being followed.

That wasn't unusual. Working here over the last year, Jock had noticed that Malcolm Evans had an ability to shut out everything around him when he wanted to.

Circumventing the front end of the car, Jock nodded a greeting at Malcolm. "Hi, boss. You had me worried. I thought maybe you weren't going to come in."

Malcolm hadn't missed a day since he'd opened, though a lot of days he'd wanted to. He knew if he gave in to that feeling, he'd never stop. He'd done that once, and it had taken him almost two years to crawl out of that black hole. "I would have called you if I wasn't going to be in."

The voice was solemn, even. Jock's father had told him that Malcolm had been the life of the party during their racing-circuit days, but Jock found it really hard to believe. He had yet to see a smile on the man. When he had once gathered enough courage to ask him about it, Malcolm had pointed out to him that Jock grinned enough for both of them.

Jock nodded toward the woman who had almost caught up to Malcolm. "Don't look now, but you're being followed."

Preoccupied with memories that had suddenly assaulted him, memories he'd been working so hard to lock away, Malcolm hadn't heard anyone walking behind him. He stopped and turned around abruptly.

Unable to stop quickly enough, Christa collided with him. Malcolm's hands went out automatically to steady her and the child she clutched to her. He'd thought he'd left her behind with the policeman who claimed to be her brother.

What was she doing following him? Their business was over.

"What?"

He bit off the question the way he might have bitten off the end of a cigar, spitting it out because it interfered with his goal. Having her anywhere around him, having the child anywhere around him, interfered with his ability to blank out his mind. To forget what only caused him pain to remember.

Christa caught herself swallowing before answering. She felt as if she was being interrogated. What *was* his problem? And why would anyone who was so obviously unfriendly put himself out to rescue her child? He was behaving like someone who didn't want to become involved. But he had.

Why?

Robin was sinking. Christa shifted her, moving the little girl up higher in her arms. "I just wanted to thank you."

"You already did." Malcolm raised his dark eyes to indicate the rear parking lot where her van was standing, buffered by two squad cars.

"I mean *really* thank you," she insisted. "Words don't seem adequate."

"Then don't waste them," he advised mildly.

With that, he turned his back on her and walked into the service area where ailing cars and the various parts that could get them up and running again were housed. In the back was a tiny alcove with a door that served as his office, a place where he retreated to when he wanted to be alone.

He was always alone now, Malcolm thought.

She had no idea what to make of him. Christa exchanged looks with the tall, gangly attendant who in turn raised wide, bony shoulders in a helpless shrug.

A car pulled up to the full-service island, and the attendant retreated. She wasn't sure if it was her imagination, but he looked somewhat relieved about it.

Christa licked her lower lip and tried again. She took a step forward, only to have Malcolm whip around, his hand raised to keep her back.

"This area's restricted," he snapped. "You could get hurt here."

Christa saw nothing that posed any immediate threat beyond the man's temperament, but she took a step back, more in reaction to his demeanor than anything else.

When she spoke, her voice was patient. "Maybe I'm not making myself clear. You just gave me back my whole life. There has to be something I can do to repay you."

Her eyes on Malcolm's face, she stroked Robin's hair to calm herself. The girl curled up against her, sucking her thumb. Her wide blue eyes were sliding closed, lulled by the soothing action.

He could remember Sally's eyes sliding closed just like that. Sally, sleeping in his arms.

Sally...

Damn it, why was he doing this to himself?

His eyes had swept over her, and a glimmer of something tender flickered in them as they rested on Robin. But when he spoke, his voice was just as gruff as it had been a moment ago.

"You could get out of the way. I've got a lot of work to do today, and you're interfering with my schedule."

Stung, confused and just a shade annoyed, Christa retreated. Emotions raw, she felt completely out of her element here. It was clear that the man couldn't be thanked. Maybe he had reacted before he thought and now regretted the whole incident. Why, she didn't know. All she knew was that, for whatever reason, he had saved Robin, and that was enough.

She nodded, turning to leave. "All right," she said quietly. "I didn't mean to intrude."

Malcolm was already leaning over the engine that had perplexed Jock. The engine he'd promised Mr. Mahoney was going to be purring by two this afternoon. "Don't let her suck her thumb too much."

The advice was carelessly tossed in her direction like a discarded gum wrapper. Surprised that he'd offered it, that he'd say anything that wasn't yanked out of him, Christa turned around to look at him again.

He never looked up, but he could feel her eyes on him just the same. He knew she was waiting for him to say something more. She'd probably stand there all day until he did.

Malcolm moved the overhead light clipped to the hood so that it illuminated the area beyond the spark plugs. "If she doesn't stop, she'll distort her palate and you'll be looking down the wrong end of a two-thousand-dollar bill for braces in about eight years."

The prediction stunned her almost as much as the man himself did. Did he have children? She glanced at the sign

to the extreme left that told her that Malcolm Evans was
the proprietor of Evans Car Service. She wondered if that
was him. Something vague, just beyond the periphery of
her thoughts, nagged at her, but she couldn't grab hold
of it.

"I'll keep that in mind." She waited, but he said
nothing else. With a perplexed sigh, Christa walked away
from the service station.

Tyler was still waiting for her when she returned to her
van. He was leaning against the hood of his car, talking
to Elliott. The other squad car was nowhere in sight.

Straightening as she approached, Tyler nodded toward the gas station. He'd watched her brief encounter
with Robin's rescuer. Body language told him that it
hadn't gone the way Christa had wanted it to.

"What was that all about?"

Christa opened the passenger side and climbed in with
Robin. All she wanted to do now was go home, sit holding Robin in her arms and forget about all this.

"I was just trying to thank him. I wanted to do something to show how very grateful I am." She shrugged as
she snapped the seat harness around Robin. "He told me
to get out of the way."

Tyler had surmised as much from the look on her face.
"Some people can't handle gratitude. They get embarrassed."

Christa climbed out again, then pulled the door shut.
She turned her face up to Tyler's. "I know, but if he
hadn't been there—"

He wouldn't let her do this to herself. She'd already
been through too much lately as it was.

"But he was." When she looked away, Tyler brack-
eted her shoulders with his hands, forcing her to raise her
eyes to his. "Don't dwell on *what ifs*, Christa. It'll drive

you crazy. You were the one who taught me that, re-member?''

She sighed. ''Yes, I remember.''

Her shoulders sagged as if all the fight had been drained from her. Tyler knew better than that, but he let his hands drop to his sides.

''We're going to need you to come down to the station and make a statement.''

Christa just wanted to put this all behind her. Being a cop's daughter, she should have realized she couldn't do that so quickly. ''Now?''

Ordinarily, he would have said yes. But this was his sister. And though she was trying to put up a brave front, he knew she was shaken. Hell, he was shaken by what had almost happened. She deserved a little slack.

''No, why don't you go home first? Take care of the bump on your head and clean up that scrape.'' Taking hold of her hand, he turned it to examine her palm. The blood was already beginning to dry. ''You can come down to the precinct later.'' She flashed a small smile in response. Even that lit up her face. It was more like the Christa he was accustomed to. ''Want me to drive you home?''

Home was a condo she had just leased last week. It was a little more than a mile down the road and still in a state of chaos, but right now, it was a haven.

She shook her head. ''No, you go do what you have to do to earn your paycheck.'' Christa saw the concern in his eyes. She placed a hand on his arm. ''I told you, I'm fine.''

Tyler could only shake his head in response. ''Stub-born as ever.''

Her eyes slanted toward the gas station. Malcolm Evans, if that was his name, was bending over the car he'd begun working on when she walked away. Its yawning hood was hanging open over him like the mouth of a shark that was getting ready to deliver a final bite.

"Yeah," she answered, "I am."

A deep, cleansing breath that helped her push aside the entire harrowing experience. She pulled open the door on the driver's side of the van and climbed in. Robin sat dozing in her seat. Poor thing, she was exhausted.

That makes two of us.

Tyler shut the door behind her. "Buckle up or I'll have to issue you a ticket."

"Bully." She slid the metal tongue into the clip. It clicked into place. "I'll be by later this afternoon, all right?"

"Whenever you're ready. Ask for Detective Harold. He'll ease you through this."

"Thanks."

As she pulled out of the parking lot, she saw her brother in her rearview mirror. He was walking over to the gas station. She wondered if he was going to have any better luck with the solemn-eyed Good Samaritan than she had had.

The police station had grown a great deal since she'd wandered the small, narrow halls as a child. Those times, she had been ushered in by her mother to visit her father at work.

A sense of pride had always shimmied through her here, even though she'd been very young. The pride had multiplied as her brothers joined the force. Christa liked the idea of them being part of what made things right in the world, part of what kept the peace.

The halls weren't narrow anymore. Renovated, the station seemed like something that belonged on the ground floor of a corporate building, not a police station. But it was a station nonetheless. A place where perpetrators were fingerprinted, where victims told their stories. It was a place where people came after bad things had happened to them.

People like her.

Christa shivered and wished she didn't have to go through this.

It could have been a lot worse, she reminded herself as she squared her shoulders.

Detective Harold was a new name to her. She'd known many of the old-timers. Her father had always brought his work home with him, cleaning up some of the coarser, uglier details as he went along. The men he worked with became a phantom part of the family.

The redheaded policewoman at the long reception desk looked up and waited expectantly as she asked, "May I help you?"

"I'm Christa Winslow. I'm here to see Detective Harold."

The policewoman rose, nodding as if she'd been expecting her. "Wait right here." She disappeared behind a wall that separated the long front reception area from the rest of the station.

Christa heard the automatic doors in the rear of the lobby open and close. Curious, she turned to see who had entered the precinct.

It was her reluctant Good Samaritan. He walked across the gleaming tiled floor, the heels of his scarred boots beating out a steady cadence, marking his approach. Even if the foyer had been crowded, she still would have singled him out. There was an aura about him.

A hundred or so years ago, people would have stopped to gawk at the stranger who rode into Dodge. He had an air of quiet power about him, power that wasn't to be challenged. He was tall and straight like a double-barreled shotgun and looked to be twice as lethal when crossed.

Something made her doubt that the appearance was deceiving.

Their eyes met at exactly the same moment, and she nodded at him. He slowly acknowledged the greeting.

She looked out of place here, Malcolm thought. She reminded him of a daisy pushing her way through a crack in the pavement.

When he reached her, she spoke first. It didn't surprise him. He wouldn't have spoken at all. The nod was enough for him.

Apparently, it wasn't enough for her.

"Hi."

Her greeting was bright, cheery, as if they were old friends rather than people who didn't even know each other's names. What was her name? Christine? Kristin? No, the policeman had called her...Christa. That was it. Christa.

He didn't have trouble recalling that the baby's name was Robin.

"Are you here to give a statement?"

Malcolm only nodded in reply. He didn't want to be here, but he couldn't very well tell that to the police. So he had worked through lunch and gotten Mahoney's car in running order, then left when the part-timer had shown up to help Jock. Though he had hoped only to have the gas station cover meager expenses, business was picking up steadily. If it continued, he was going to have to hire more help. The thought didn't please him. The fewer people he had to interact with, the better.

Christa remembered what he'd said to her earlier. "I guess this is really interfering with your schedule." Again, he nodded. Why couldn't he say something? Nerves sharply cut through the veneer of politeness she was attempting to maintain. "You know, they're going to ask you to talk."

The way annoyance appeared and then disappeared across her brow amused him. His mouth curved just the slightest bit.

"I'll talk," he answered quietly.

He *could* smile. The sight of it softened her. "I'm sorry about all this."

It hadn't occurred to him to hold her accountable for the inconvenience. He'd chosen to pursue the fleeing van; she hadn't forced him to do it.

"Not your fault."

She blew out a breath. "I know, but if you hadn't come to my rescue, to Robin's rescue—"

"Then things would be a lot more serious than they are now." He saw another apology or exclamation of everlasting gratitude hovering on her lips. He wanted neither. "Forget it."

It was a curt command, but she wasn't about to obey. "I can't," she insisted, vehemently enough to catch his attention. "I can't forget it. What happened today could have changed my life forever. It could have changed Robin's life forever. Or ended it. You prevented that. It's not something I can just push out of my mind." She paused only for a moment, searching his face. "Why won't you let me thank you?"

Malcolm didn't want to get into it with her. He looked past the blond head, searching for someone to give his name to and get this all over with. But there was no one behind the long ebony-and-chrome desk.

"Let's just say that this was a small payment on a debt I owe."

His answer baffled her. She found herself wanting to make sense out of it. "I don't understand."

He shook his head, dismissing her part in it. "That's all right. You weren't involved."

There were no landmarks to help her pick her way through the maze. She didn't like being lost. It was clear to her that he was carrying on some inner conversation with himself that she was only accidentally privy to. It was a subject that obviously caused him pain. Because of what he'd done for her, for Robin, she was determined to learn more.

The policewoman chose that moment to return. "If you follow me, I'll take you to Detective Harold." She raised her eyes to Malcolm's face.

"I'm Malcolm Evans. Officer McGuire told me to come in to give my statement regarding—"

She nodded. "Detective Simms is waiting to see you. Why don't you both come around the desk and follow me inside?"

Malcolm stepped back and gestured for Christa to go first.

Malcolm Evans. So that had been his name on the sign earlier. Ever since she'd read it, the name had been teasing her. She'd heard it before, though the connection eluded her. It flittered back and forth in her mind like an annoying gnat.

The policewoman ushered them to two adjacent desks in the squad room before disappearing.

For the next twenty minutes, Christa and Malcolm gave their statements to two detectives. Detective Harold questioned Christa about the incident as gently as if he were dealing with his own daughter. She discovered that he had known her father. She answered his questions as completely as she could, all the while trying to listen to what Malcolm was telling Detective Simms. She succeeded only minimally.

Detective Harold offered her the paper he had just finished typing. Glancing over it, she signed her name on the bottom.

Christa laid the pen down. "Is that all?"

"No." Tyler's voice came from behind her. "Now you have to pick him out of a lineup."

She offered an apologetic smile as she rose to her feet. "Sorry, I would have known that if it wasn't happening to me."

"Don't worry about it." Tyler slipped an arm around her shoulders. "Who's baby-sitting? Dad?" She nodded. "You know, he makes a much nicer grandfather than he did a father."

Christa laughed. "Sometimes these things take time. Dad's a late bloomer." A stern disciplinarian, her father had turned into a pushover with Robin.

"Almost finished?" Tyler asked the burly man at the next desk.

In response, the detective took out a pen and handed it to Malcolm. "Just needs a signature."

But Malcolm was in no hurry to sign. Instead, he slowly read through the words the older man had typed on the form.

Tyler laid a hand on Malcolm's shoulder. "We'll wait for you in the hall." The question was silent, evident in the set of the wide shoulders. "We're going to need your ID, as well—separately," Tyler explained.

Malcolm only nodded in response. Tyler ushered Christa into the hall.

"So, how did it go?"

"Pretty painless. Detective Harold's nice—just like you said."

"Nothing but the best for my baby sister."

Christa looked toward the glass encompassed squad room. Malcolm was signing the bottom of the form. "Do your baby sister a favor?"

He knew better than to say yes right away. "What?"

"Can you get me some information on him?"

Tyler didn't have to ask who "him" was. It was against the rules to give out information on the forms, but some rules could be bent on occasion, and this seemed a harmless enough infraction.

"Why?"

"I have a feeling I know him, or of him, from somewhere." She saw the skepticism in Tyler's eyes. He probably thought she had other reasons for asking. Maybe she did.

Christa had never been the type to drift through life, Tyler knew. She had to be an active player and turn everyone around her into one, as well. "Isn't it enough that he was there at the right place at the right time?"

She shook her head. "It's because he was that I want to know." She looked toward Malcolm thoughtfully. "There's something bothering him."

Tyler frowned. As if she didn't have enough problems to deal with as an out-of-work single mother with a small daughter to raise and a deadbeat ex-husband who would never make any child-support payments. "There's something bothering all of us, Christa."

"I know, but—"

Humoring her, he kissed the top of her head. "Okay, I'll see what I can do," he promised.

She grinned up at him. "I never doubted it for a minute."

Chapter Three

It was past four o'clock when Malcolm finally walked out of the police station. As he hurried down the stone stairs that led to the parking lot, he noted that the lot had thinned out considerably. There was only a smattering of cars left. Business at the police station had to be slacking off, he mused.

Walking toward the black sports car, he became aware of the grating, whining noise. It was a sound he was more than passingly familiar with. Metal on metal, sparking nothing but aggravation as it prophesied a stranded motorist.

Malcolm automatically glanced in the direction the noise was originating from.

He might have known.

It was coming from her van.

His initial impulse was to ignore the sound, and her, and just keep walking. That would have been the sensible thing to do.

MARIE FERRARELLA   37

Malcolm got as far as the driver's side of his own car before he finally turned around. The grinding noise put his teeth on edge as she tried to turn the ignition on again. He couldn't just drive away and leave her like this. In a vague way, it was tantamount to a fireman ignoring a fire alarm or a policeman ignoring a cry for help.

He'd thought that she would be gone by the time he was finished at the station. Her brother and another policeman had led Christa in first to look at the men in the line up. It had taken her all of one minute to pick out the man who had car-jacked her van.

It had taken him a little less than three minutes to make the same choice. Malcolm had deliberately taken his time after that, hoping she'd be gone when he walked out of the station.

Obviously, he hadn't taken enough time.

She was going to kill that thing if she didn't stop. By his count, she'd tried to start the van six times since he'd left the building.

"C'mon, c'mon, start," Christa chanted under her breath. The mantra wasn't working. The engine refused to turn over.

She turned the key again just before he reached her. The window on her side was open, and he heard her mumbling something under her breath, but he couldn't make it out. The grinding noise drowned it out.

"You'll flood the engine."

Christa started, her head jerking up at the sound of someone at her elbow. When she saw it was Malcolm, she relaxed, but not before the exasperated sigh escaped her lips.

"Right about now, I'd like to drown the engine."

Malcolm nodded. It had been a long time since a car's problems had baffled him, but he could relate to the helplessness she had to be experiencing.

It was the way he had felt about life when he had found himself alive in the hospital bed. Alive when Gloria and Sally were gone.

Christa threw up her hands in surrender. She'd been trying to start the van for the past ten minutes. Taking every curve life had to throw at her, Christa prided herself on being levelheaded and calm. Today, however, her nerves were very close to the surface.

She looked at him. "Any suggestions?"

In reply, Malcolm circled the front of her van and placed his hands on the hood. Then, as she watched, mystified, he pushed down on it, hard. She felt the vehicle begin to bounce up and down like a small sailboat caught in a storm at sea.

He wasn't behaving like any mechanic she knew. Christa stuck her head out the window. "What are you doing?"

Malcolm didn't bother answering. Instead, he gave her an order. "Now try it." When she just looked at him, he added, "Turn the key."

Not seeing how what he was doing could make any difference whatsoever, Christa turned the key in the ignition. She was rewarded with the sound of the engine turning over. The van vibrated as the engine coughed to life, shuddering like a wet dog.

Relief coaxed a grin from her. "Is that the auto mechanic's equivalent of a TV repairman hitting the side of a set when it doesn't work?"

The principle would take too much effort to explain to her. "Something like that." He cocked his head, listening to the sound of the engine as it idled. A starter motor wasn't her only problem. The engine sounded as if it was wheezing, and the car was idling rough. Besides that, he detected the light scent of gasoline.

Not my business, he thought.

But cars *were* his business. If he let her go now and she wound up stranded somewhere, it would be partially his fault. A great deal had changed in his life, but Malcolm still believed that omission was just as much of a sin as commission.

Trapped by his conscience, he reluctantly asked, "You live far from here?"

The nice thing about the condo she was leasing was that it was so centrally located. "A couple of miles." She nodded toward the street right off the parking lot. "West Plaza Development. Just off Heather."

Heather Drive. That was in the opposite direction from his own apartment. Malcolm sighed. He supposed it wouldn't be too far out of his way. "All right, I'll follow you home."

Now, that was a switch. Though she appreciated it, she didn't see any reason for his abrupt change of heart. "Any particular reason you've suddenly decided to become friendly?"

Malcolm sniffed the air. Nothing. The light scent of gasoline must have just been his imagination.

"I'm not being friendly," he corrected mildly. "I'm being a mechanic. I don't like the sound of your engine. You might not make it home."

"I hate putting you out like this."

That made two of them. He shrugged in reply. "Like you said, you live only a couple of miles down the road. No big deal."

That sounded more like him, Christa thought. Distant. Matter-of-fact. And he was wrong; it *was* a big deal.

She was a stranger and he was offering to help. Again. She felt bound to tell him the absolute truth.

"It's not exactly two miles. More like five," she amended.

Two, five—it made no difference. He had already made the offer.

"Five," he repeated, accepting the correction. Malcolm glanced at his watch. "We're still not quite into rush hour yet. Shouldn't take more than ten minutes to reach your house." The idling sound the van was making was beginning to sound like someone with smoker's hack. "Unless, of course, the van breaks down," he added matter-of-factly. "I'm parked two aisles over." He jerked his thumb toward the LeMans. "Wait for me."

It was more of an order than anything else.

He was one strange man, she thought. There was something about him that spoke to her. Despite his size and the aura of power he cast, there was something about him that was reaching out to her. She doubted if he was even aware of it.

Tyler would have said she was meddling.

Mentally, Christa crossed her fingers as she backed out of her space. The van seemed to shimmy and shudder more than usual. She had the impression that it was like a prize-winning stallion past its peak, trying to eke out just a little more life before it died.

She kept her fingers crossed all the way home. The van didn't die, but Christa had the uneasy feeling that it was touch and go all the way. It was reassuring to see the LeMans in her rearview mirror.

The van had over a hundred and fifty thousand miles on it. It had brought her safely over the desert, when she had left with Las Vegas and Jim in her rearview mirror. Actually, she amended silently, only Las Vegas had been in her rearview mirror. Jim, at the time of her departure, had probably been housed somewhere at a casino table, hoping that Lady Luck had decided not to snub him any longer.

Luck had been an elusive, capricious partner during the five years that she and Jim had been married. When she'd had enough of his gambling fever and divorced him, he'd acted relieved. He'd called Christa his Jonah. Without her, he felt confident that his luck would change for the better.

She sincerely doubted it, but she was decent enough to hope that it had. No matter what, the man would always be Robin's father. That meant something.

All during the trip back to Southern California, she'd had the uneasy feeling that she was on borrowed time. Each false start and stop that the van made only increased that feeling. Today's harrowing chase down Bedford's main thoroughfare had undoubtedly wreaked havoc on the failing engine.

Or whatever it was that was wrong with the van, she mused with resignation.

Just last a little longer. Please.

Finally, Christa pulled up in the short driveway in front of her condo. Malcolm's car was only a beat behind her. Though there was ample room in the driveway, he parked in the street, directly in front of her father's vintage Jaguar.

She watched Malcolm smoothly guide his car into the tight space between her father's car and her neighbor's. Admiration curved her lips. She couldn't conceive of doing that. She could no more manage to parallel-park than she could fly on her own power.

Malcolm slammed the car door shut behind him. He nodded at the dark metallic green Jaguar. Her husband must be the sporty type, he decided.

"Nice car. Yours?"

She shook her head. With a bank account barely in the triple digits, she could ill afford maintenance on something like that.

"My father's." She smiled, thinking of the way he pampered the vehicle. "It's his baby now that he's retired."

Malcolm nodded absently, acutely aware that she had turned her electric blue eyes up at him. He didn't quite know what he was doing here. He was going out of his way, and he'd made it a practice never to go out of his way. The less involved he was with people in general, the less there would be to trigger him, to remind him of what he no longer had.

Of what he had allowed, because of a momentary lapse in skill, to slip through his fingers.

Feeling uncomfortable, Malcolm slowly shoved wide, capable hands into his back pockets. He stood looking at her van.

Now would be the time to back out. Before he got in too deep.

"Well, you got here without any mishaps. Maybe your husband could take a look at the van for you."

He was already turning to go when he saw the amused smile rising to her lips. It feathered up to her eyes. The sight was appealing, though Malcolm didn't want it to be.

She could just see Jim staring into the interior of the engine. He would have been more lost than her.

"I don't have a husband, at least, not anymore. And when I did have one, he would have been far more prone to look at a deck of cards than a car. Jim wasn't what you'd call handy by any stretch of the imagination.''

What he had been, she thought, was a spinner of dreams. Unattainable, impossible dreams. They'd been magical once. But the magic had long since faded from his dreams and their life together.

Malcolm gave no indication that he had heard her or absorbed the information she offered. But he did approach the van with a resigned expression on his face.

He was here, he thought, so he might as well take a look at it. "Pop the hood for me."

Obediently, Christa pulled the lever on the dashboard. The hood made a noise as it rose an inch, still tethered to a lock.

Feeling around for the release latch, Malcolm found it and pulled. He moved the hood back and looked in, letting out a long, low whistle. That had to be one of the dirtiest engines he'd seen in a long, long time. And just possibly the worst cared for. He shook his head.

Christa joined him and looked down below the yawning hood. She had absolutely no idea what she was looking at, other than the fact that there was a great deal of metal and rubber snaking into itself that she didn't begin to understand.

She was standing too close to him. The light scent she wore somehow managed to block out the smell of gasoline that was now much more prevalent since she had opened the hood. He wished she would move.

"So, what's the prognosis, Doctor?" Her voice was teasing as she crossed her arms before her. "Can the patient be saved?"

Not without a hell of a lot of work, he thought. Malcolm looked at her, trying to gauge just how knowledgeable she was. "How much do you know about cars?"

That was an easy one. "You put the key in and they go?" she offered with an apologetic shrug that should have irked him but did just the opposite.

He laughed very softly, but she heard him and it warmed her.

"Not this time," he said. The hoses all looked worn. A couple of them were cracked. And he'd been right about that smell of gasoline. She had a leak somewhere. His guess was that one of the seals on the fuel injectors was cracked.

"You're lucky to have gotten home. From the sound of it, I'd say that your starter motor has just about had it and I'm surprised that you're getting anything out of your battery." He indicated the corroded couplings. "The cables are completely corroded with residue. By all rights, there shouldn't even be a connection being made."

He wasn't even going to bother getting into the hoses and the fuel injectors, except to warn her. "I wouldn't drive it if I were you. There's a faint smell of gasoline. It's not safe."

Christa wrinkled her nose; she believed Malcolm's assessment. She knew she'd been pushing her luck with the van, but she'd had no choice. A new one, or even a new used one, was out of the question right now.

"Can you fix it?"

He felt as if she had just placed a wounded baby bird in his lap and asked him to breathe life into it.

"Well, it needs a new starter motor, and there's no telling what else might be wrong with it—"

This was beginning to sound worse and worse. "So it won't be fixed by tomorrow?"

Did she think he was a miracle worker? He began to say just that, then decided against it. "No, it won't be fixed by tomorrow."

Christa sighed, dragging her hand through her hair. "Oh, God."

She sounded as if he'd just told her the car was terminal. "Is tomorrow important?"

"It might have been." She dug deep, trying to rally her sinking spirit, but it wasn't getting any easier. "I have a job interview. Had," she amended. "I was counting on getting there with this." She waved a disparaging hand at the van.

"Not unless the place interviewing you is located at the bottom of a hill."

Christa nibbled on her lower lip again, thinking. Watching her stirred a distant feeling in Malcolm that he had been certain had completely vanished from his life the day he'd buried Gloria.

He pushed it away.

Christa knew she had no right to impose. But she was desperate. "Could you work on it for me?"

Malcolm had never seen so much hope in a woman's eyes before. Unfounded hope, he thought, but hope nonetheless. It pinned him to the spot and kept him there. It also gave him no choice.

Shrugging, he acquiesced. "Sure. I could have it towed to the shop—"

Towing. Something else to consider. "Is that going to cost?" Before he could answer, she flushed ruefully. "Of course it's going to cost."

She ran a slender hand over her face. God, but it was hard not to feel as if her back were against the wall. She knew she could always turn to her brothers and father for money, but her pride wouldn't let her.

"It was a stupid question." Looking at him, she tried to explain what had caused her to blurt it out. "It's just that I've budgeted everything down to the penny. Most

of my money went into securing the lease on this house.
Anything extra—there wasn't much—I earmarked for
Robin's birthday. She's going to be two at the end of the
month.'' And she really wanted to make it special for her.
They both needed that.

The woman was tugging at feelings that he wanted to
leave untouched. Malcolm felt as if the words were being dragged out of him.

"I suppose I could work on it here." As soon as he said
that, he saw her eyes light up. It was like standing in the
midst of magic. She really did think he could perform
miracles, he realized.

She hated being crass, but money was a definite ob-
ject here. She had to ask. Christa didn't want him working on the van if she couldn't pay him.

"How much do you think it'll run? The starter engine," she clarified.

"Motor," he corrected.

"Motor," Christa repeated. Her error didn't faze her.
"And your labor, of course."

The woman was the last word in naivete, he thought.
An unscrupulous mechanic's dream come true. They'd
see her coming a mile away.

Something protective took over before he could stop it.

Malcolm ran a hand along the back of his neck. He
was getting in deeper than he had wanted to, but there
didn't seem to be a good way of turning her down. Not
when she was so obviously in dire straits. If he did, he'd
have her on his conscience.

There was enough on his conscience already.

"We'll work something out," he promised with a resigned sigh.

She wasn't about to accept charity. She wasn't going to accept it from her family, and she was even less inclined to accept it from a stranger.

"I will pay you," she promised fiercely. "In the meantime, you're a saint."

His eyes darkened, fathomless and dangerous. "We'll work something out on one condition."

Christa drew a breath and held it. "Yes?"

"That you don't deify me and you don't keep thanking me." It went beyond making him uncomfortable. It just wasn't true.

She still didn't understand him. Twice he'd come to her aid and then gotten angry when she reacted. "Under the circumstances, punching you out just doesn't seem to fit the occasion."

He could feel his mouth curving involuntarily. "One 'thank you' will do."

The smile on her lips was inviting. "I'll give it my best shot."

It wasn't a game. He was serious. "Those are my terms."

She nodded. "I understand." She didn't, but that was beside the point. There were bigger things to concern her at the moment. "Now all I have to do is find a way to get to the interview tomorrow morning."

He turned away from her, but not before he saw the hopeful look reenter her eyes again. "How about your father?" he asked.

She shook her head. "I'll need him to stay with Robin."

That wasn't what he had meant. He was talking about the Jaguar. "But his car isn't going to be in the living room with him."

Christa laughed. She'd sooner ask her father to go to the interview in her place than ask him to lend her his precious car. "Dad loves me, but he doesn't let anyone else drive the Jaguar, and he's not about to start now."

"Then I'd say you have yourself a problem."

She didn't ask, but he could see that she wanted to. It was there, in her eyes, as plain as if it were written down on a page. She was hoping he'd offer to take her. Well, she could hope for that from now until hell froze over. He was already putting himself out more than he had ever intended on doing.

A hell of a lot more than he knew he should.

"Yes," she agreed quietly. "I guess I do."

Her quiet tone bothered him almost as much as the look in her eyes, and there was no reason either should.

He had to be getting back, before he did something else he'd wind up regretting.

Malcolm slid in behind the wheel of his car. "I'll be back to take a look at your van later this evening," he told her. "After I close up." The gas station remained open all night, but the garage closed its doors at seven. A man needed some time to himself.

She nodded, then hurried over to his car just as he was about to pull away from the curb. *Now what?* he thought.

"Dinner?" She shot the word out as if she were guessing the answer to a clue on a game show.

"What?"

Tyler always said she talked faster than most people thought. "Can I at least make you dinner tonight? To thank you—silently," Christa added.

He eased his foot off the brake and onto the accelerator, amused despite himself as she trotted along beside him down the block. "I thought you said you were on a budget."

She glanced up the block to make sure there was no car coming into the cul-de-sac.

"There's always room for one more. Besides, feeding you will cost a lot less than having the car towed to your garage." She could see that he was about to refuse. "Please? It'll make me feel better." She stopped in the middle of the street. The LeMans continued to the corner. Christa raised her voice. "I don't like being in debt."

Well, they had that much in common. Though he guessed that she probably couldn't see him, he shrugged carelessly in response to her question. It was easier than arguing with her.

"We'll see," he muttered.

Christa stood in the street, watching him drive away. He could see her in his rearview mirror. The woman didn't even have enough sense to come out of the street, he snorted with a shake of his head.

Damn, what the hell had he allowed himself to get sucked into?

By the time he reached his garage, Malcolm had made his decision. He was going to cancel, both on dinner and the repair job. He'd give her the name of another reputable mechanic.

Let her be someone else's headache, not his.

His plan was spoiled by the fact that he didn't have Christa's telephone number. When he called directory assistance, he was informed that her number was unlisted. His choices were to either not show up or drive by and tell her in person that he had changed his mind.

He didn't care for either.

Carefully, he lowered the engine he had rebuilt into the cavernous chassis. He had more than enough work to keep him busy. He sure as hell didn't have time to play nursemaid to a woman with huge electric blue eyes and a way of stirring him up.

More than that, he had no time to get involved in anyone else's problems. Malcolm had a feeling that to be around Christa Winslow for any amount of time was just asking for trouble, and he'd had more than his share of that.

Malcolm wiped his hands on a rag and began tightening bolts carefully. If he had wanted to socialize, he thought, working his way around the perimeter of the engine, he could always pick up the telephone and call any one of a number of people he'd turned away in the past three years. People who had once been his friends.

People he kept at a distance now.

His refusal mapped out, he decided to call it a day. Locking up the work area, Malcolm nodded a good-night to Sam, the man who worked the late-night shift, and got into his car.

He'd stop by, tell her he'd changed his mind and that would be that. All things considered, he'd probably be home in another fifteen minutes. In time to heat up another solitary meal in the microwave and go through his mail before he turned on the news.

Chapter Four

The tersely worded refusal Malcolm intended to give Christa was there, on the tip of his tongue and ready for launch as he drove up along the pine-tree-lined cul-de-sac. When he guided his car to the end of the block, the time was T-minus-1 and counting.

And then the mission was scrubbed.

The warm July evening had brought her out of her modest white stucco-and-wood condo. He had the impression that Christa was oblivious to everything around her except the little girl she was playing with. Malcolm slowed the car down to barely a crawl as he watched them together.

Christa was wearing the shortest pair of white denim shorts he'd seen in a very long time. That and a white-and-lime-striped tank top that was glued to her torso thanks to the layer of perspiration that glistened like stardust all along her body.

She wore her clothes not like a woman who had intentionally set out to allure anyone but like a woman who'd carelessly tossed on the first things she'd grabbed. She looked comfortable in them, which made her that much more alluring. Because none of the effect was calculated.

Although different in coloring, stature and temperament, she still reminded him of Gloria.

The evening wasn't particularly hot, but Christa had worked up a sweat chasing after Robin. The little girl seemed to be made out of pure energy.

Robin would sleep like a rock tonight, Christa thought. At least that would make one of them. After what she'd been through today, Christa felt too wound up to sleep.

"I'm going to get you," Christa warned with a laugh. She grabbed for Robin and missed intentionally.

With a squeal of delight, Robin went tumbling down the slight grassy incline that made up the front lawn, rolling like a ball. Her laughter, light and airy, filled the still air.

It was the laughter that got to Malcolm, echoing in his mind and filling his soul. It affected him just as much as the sight of the woman did.

For a brief moment, he forgot—forced himself to forget—the pain the memories stirred and just dug down deep for the joy. The joy of playing with his little girl. The joy of loving his wife. The joy he'd felt just treasuring the simple things.

Because he'd lived so long with death riding over his shoulder during his racing career, Malcolm had learned to always live his life to the fullest off the track. It became almost a mandate, especially when he began to win the races he entered.

Initially that meant partying every night, with no holds barred. And then he'd found and fallen in love with Gloria, and living life to the fullest took on a whole new meaning and direction.

For such a very limited amount of time.

With iron resolve, he shook himself free of the past. Pressing down on the accelerator again, he swung the car around until it faced the cross street.

Christa scooped Robin up in her arms as the little girl tumbled to the grass's edge. She turned, still laughing, when she heard the car approach.

Seven-fifteen. She'd begun to think that perhaps he wasn't coming. There was no real reason for Malcolm Evans to keep his word. After all, she was really nothing to him.

But something inside Christa had resisted giving up hope. That was the one thing that had always kept her going, even through her darker times. Hope. The belief that things were going to turn around, that they were going to be better and soon.

Looking at the up side of everything was the only way she knew how to live.

Positioning Robin so that the little girl was comfortably straddling her right hip, Christa moved her damp bangs away from her forehead with the back of her hand. She winced as she came in contact with the bump. It was still very tender. She moved her hair back in place and grinned at Malcolm.

"Hi."

"Hi!" Robin chirped, brightly echoing her mother's greeting like a twenty-pound blond parakeet.

"Hi," Malcolm murmured, more to the child than the woman.

Because of who he was, what he was and what he'd once been, the choice to leave had been completely taken away with that single greeting.

Telling himself he was going to really regret this, Malcolm parked his car just short of Christa's driveway. As he got out of the LeMans, he noticed that the Jaguar wasn't there anymore.

"Father gone?"

She nodded, a large grin sprouting on a mouth that seemed too generous for her face and yet somehow suited her.

"He has a date tonight." Mentally, Christa crossed her fingers for her father. It was a blind date that Tyler had arranged for him. June Lee was the widowed mother of one of the other officers. It was her father's first date in years.

Malcolm saw no reason why she should share this piece of information with him or why the thought of her father going through the awkward scenario of a date should give her so much pleasure.

"Your mother know?" He wondered if her parents were divorced and surprised himself with the speculation. It had been a long time since he had wondered anything personal about anyone.

Out of habit, Christa glanced up toward the sky. If Martha McGuire couldn't be with them, Christa liked the idea of her mother looking down and watching over all of them.

"Actually, I think she had a hand in arranging it. Dad says she's been looking after him ever since she passed away."

He hadn't meant to touch on anything that personal. "Sorry."

Christa saw the sharp stab of pain that flashed over his face and kicked herself for inadvertently treading on his wounds. She knew he was a widower. Tyler, true to his promise, had gotten back to her an hour after she'd arrived home. The information he gave her was sketchy, but it had told Christa at least some of what she wanted to know. She also knew now why Malcolm had seemed so familiar to her.

"Don't be," she told him easily. "You didn't know." With the agility of a boneless child, Robin suddenly lunged forward, making a grab for Malcolm, taking them both by surprise. Christa pulled back. "No, Robin, don't."

But it was too late. Robin had managed to snag the edge of Malcolm's shirt. A button was ripped loose and went flying.

Great, she thought.

Christa watched to see where the button landed. "I'll sew that back on," she promised quickly, moving to pick it up.

He shrugged the incident off. "Don't bother. I'll take care of it."

Christa didn't bother to hide her amusement as she looked down at his large, wide hands. She couldn't picture him holding a needle.

"You sew?"

"I can push a needle back and forth." There didn't seem to be much talent called for in that. His brows narrowed as he looked at her. She'd made an assumption with her offer. "What makes you think I'm not married?"

If she told him how she knew, she'd have to admit that she'd had Tyler do a little digging about him. Christa had a strong feeling that Malcolm wouldn't have liked that.

He seemed to be much too private a person to welcome intruders, no matter how innocent or well-meaning.

"Um, because if you were, you would have told me that your wife doesn't like you having dinner with strange women when I invited you earlier."

Nice save, she congratulated herself silently. Christa watched his face to see if he bought her explanation. His expression was unreadable.

After a beat, Malcolm nodded, letting her reasoning pass. "You pick up on things quickly."

Relieved, she smiled at him as Robin wound stubby, grass-stained fingers into her hair. "I try."

He wondered if the little girl was ever still. She seemed like unharnessed energy temporarily captured in a small container.

Malcolm glanced back at the van. He noticed that Christa hadn't bothered closing the hood after he had left. "Then tell me, why wouldn't a savvy woman like you take your car in for maintenance?"

Being a mechanic, he probably wouldn't understand, but she told him anyway. "With everything else happening in my life, it wasn't very high on my priority list."

That much was obvious. "Given the state of the van, I'd say it wasn't on it at all."

"Then you'd be right." Trying to get Jim to grow up and take on some responsibility had taken precedence over everything else.

"Oil changes?" The question was perfunctory. Malcolm felt he already had the answer to that one.

She shook her head, not quite following him. Gritting her teeth, she barely kept from wincing as Robin tugged harder. Christa pulled her daughter's busy fingers out of her hair.

"Excuse me?"

Malcolm nodded at the vehicle on her driveway. "When did you last have the oil changed?"

She paused, thinking. For the life of her, she couldn't remember.

Just as he suspected. Malcolm shook his head. "Never mind."

Feeling as if she had flunked some initial pop quiz, Christa set Robin down on the ground. Still holding on to her daughter's hand, she bent over to pick up the button before it was lost or Robin decided that it was some kind of new candy and popped it into her mouth.

Malcolm tried not to watch as the cuffs of Christa's shorts hitched up so high on her legs that it would have made a man's mouth water.

If a man was hungry.

His gut tightened. Even if he wasn't hungry, he thought. Christa tucked the button into the pocket of her shorts. He could have sworn that there wasn't room there to tuck in a spare breath.

"Man," Robin announced, pointing at Malcolm.

Yes, he certainly is, Christa thought. *With a capital M.*

"Man," Robin repeated, this time more insistently as she raised her arms to him and waited expectantly for him to respond.

"I think she wants you to pick her up," Christa prompted. Watching his expression, she wondered how he would react.

Christa saw the hesitation in his eyes. He seemed torn between gruffly dismissing the little girl and giving in to what Christa guessed was a real desire to hold the child.

He wanted to hold her but he didn't. Why? And what was the source of the pain she saw?

She wanted to come to his aid and then realized that she really didn't know how. To help him, she had to know what he was feeling and why. She doubted very much if he would let her know.

Robin stamped a tiny, sneakered foot on the concrete, raising her hands higher. *"Man."*

"Demanding little female, isn't she?" he commanded.

Christa began to apologize, then stopped. He wasn't looking for an apology. The hard edges of his features had softened as he looked down at her daughter.

Malcolm laughed quietly at the serious look on the rosebud mouth and round cheeks. Before he could reason himself out of it, he bent down to the girl's level and picked her up. She smelled vaguely of chocolate and grass. And heaven.

"This what you want?"

The blond head bobbed up and down.

Christa held her tongue, and her breath, as she watched them together. They belonged, she thought. Two halves of a puzzle. A man without a child and a child without a father. It was almost as if they were made for each other.

Was he someone's father? she wondered.

The next moment, Robin patted his face in approval with small, pudgy hands. Pleased, guileless, childish laughter filled the air. "Man."

Christa looked at Malcolm's cheek where Robin had patted him. And left her mark.

Terrific, now she's gotten him dirty.

"I think she's branded you." Gently but firmly, Christa extracted a squirming Robin, taking her back into her arms.

Malcolm quirked a brow at her comment. In response, Christa ran her finger lightly along his cheek where the small splotch of chocolate ice cream marked his skin.

Her breath locked in her throat at the dark, smoldering look that came into his eyes. The air around her turned overwhelmingly sultry. She dropped her hand to her side as if it had touched a red-hot poker.

"Um, she had chocolate ice cream a few minutes ago," Christa heard herself explaining, though she didn't remember forming the words. "I thought I got it all, but I must have missed some."

He could still feel the imprint of both the child and the woman on his skin. It felt indelible.

The hint of a smile that Robin had coaxed from him left abruptly as he turned his back on them. "I'd better get started."

Christa remained rooted to the ground. She hesitated for a moment, wanting to say something. Common sense warned her not to.

But for a second back there, she had felt something, something dark and exciting. Something almost electric. Had he felt it, as well? Or was that just her imagination going into overdrive?

She licked her suddenly dry lips. "Then we'd better get out of your way."

He didn't bother looking at her. Malcolm went to his car and took out the toolbox he had brought with him from the garage. As he did, he realized that he had set himself up. He wouldn't have thrown the hoses and the tools into his car if he had really meant to turn her down.

He'd meant to do this all along.

He might be willing to help her, but that didn't mean he had to put up with having her hang around. He'd always worked better alone.

"I'd appreciate it."

He would, she thought sadly. He seemed the type who preferred walking through life alone. She could understand that to an extent. She'd felt the same when she had come to her decision about Jim.

But with all her heart, she believed that it wasn't good for people to be alone with whatever hurts they harbored. People weren't meant to behave like animals, to retreat beneath a table or into a cave to lick their wounds until they healed.

Christa glanced over her shoulder at Malcolm before going into the house. She wished that Tyler could have gotten her just a little more information.

The July sky had turned dusky, the western horizon painted in the fading purple hues of evening. The street lamp just outside her house had turned on half an hour ago and was now illuminating the area far better than the crescent moon did.

Christa had fed and bathed Robin and put her to bed, then read to her. They had gotten as far as the three little pigs venturing out into the world to seek their fortunes before Robin's wide blue eyes had drifted shut.

It had been a very long day for both of them, Christa thought, tiptoeing out.

When she came into the living room and crossed to her window, Christa half expected not to see Malcolm. He'd be the type to leave without saying a word.

But he was still there, working by the light of the street lamp and the fixture he'd brought with him, which was now clipped to the inside of her hood.

He'd been at it for over two hours.

The man was dedicated; there was no doubt about that. Guilt nibbled at her. There had to be some way she could show him her appreciation that he wouldn't just shove back at her.

Christa debated going out. She knew he'd rather she remained in the house until he was finished. Or, barring that, until he left, stealing off into the night like the Lone Mechanic.

She grinned at the imagery. She didn't want him to just leave. And she didn't want him to work into the wee hours of the night, either.

Making up her mind, she walked outside. Dusk wrapped its arms around her as she approached Malcolm. It helped soothe the inexplicable jumpiness she was experiencing.

He heard her.

Immersed in his work, he could still hear the soft tread of her approach as her bare feet padded along the cooling concrete walk. Involuntarily, Malcolm glanced over his shoulder.

She was still wearing that flimsy excuse for an outfit. He would have thought that she would have changed by now.

He turned back to his work and continued reconnecting the battery. His elbow jostled the toothbrush he'd used to clean the cables, and it fell to the driveway.

"Something wrong?" he asked mildly when she didn't say anything. It seemed out of character for her to be quiet.

She picked up the toothbrush, setting it on the bumper. "Yes, you're working too long."

He'd lost track of time, only vaguely aware that the sun had completely slipped away. "I'm not finished." He wouldn't be, of course. The van had a great many things that needed attention, but he'd set a goal for tonight, and it hadn't been met yet.

He hadn't allowed for Christa in his schedule.

Battery reconnected, Malcolm straightened and flexed the cramped muscles in his shoulders and neck. He sighed. Maybe it was time to call it a night.

"And I won't be finished," he added for her benefit. "At least, not tonight."

He began to wipe his hands on the back of his jeans. Christa offered him a towel that looked much too clean to handle the grease he'd accumulated.

He declined the towel. "It'll get dirty."

She pushed the small kitchen towel into his hands. "It's a towel. Getting dirty is its job."

With a shake of his head, he took it, cleaning off the dirt as best he could. It wasn't enough. What he needed was some good industrial hand soap, he thought.

Giving her back the towel, Malcolm glanced at the pile of cracked, worn hoses that lay like a rubber funeral pyre on the curb. By all rights, her van should have died a long time ago.

"I can't figure how your van kept going all this time."

She smiled at him brightly, as guilelessly as her daughter had. It had the same effect on him.

"I guess my luck held up, at least in this department." She patted the side of the hood as if the vehicle were a pet instead of just metal and rubber bumpers. "If this had died in the desert—"

Malcolm stared at her in disbelief. Talk about being foolhardy. How could she have risked something like that? Only an idiot would have taken an old vehicle like this on an extended trip without checking it out first. "You took it to the desert?"

He made it sound as if she'd committed a cardinal sin. "Only way to get here from Las Vegas unless you're flying." Her mouth quirked. "And it's hard to pack all your possessions into the overhead luggage rack." A rueful smile blossomed. "Although, I have to admit that I didn't have all that much more to transport. Mostly Robin's things."

She was giving him much more information than he wanted. And yet it sparked a desire for more.

He squelched it.

But it was hard to make idle conversation without asking some questions. Malcolm surrendered. "So you moved here recently?"

Around them, crickets were engaged in a concert. The chirping sounded like a serenade. With the darkness enveloping them, the evening became warmly intimate. Malcolm tried to ignore that.

She nodded. "Three weeks ago. I stayed with my father until I could find a place for us." She turned to look at him. "I'm divorced."

She said it as if she were a veteran of a war. Turning from her, Malcolm scooped up the worn hoses he'd removed from her car and dumped them into his car. "I didn't ask."

Christa followed him. "I know. I just like saying it."

Malcolm looked at her over his shoulder, waiting for an explanation. She didn't hesitate in giving it.

"Shows that even I know when I've made a mistake." She tucked her thumbs through the belt loops of her shorts and rocked on the balls of her bare feet. "Tyler says I always hang on, no matter what, even when I'm wrong. But even I knew that I had made a mistake marrying Jim."

She had resisted admitting it to herself for a long time. It had taken her a while to realize that admitting that her marriage was a mistake didn't necessarily mean that everything about it had been. If she hadn't married Jim, she would have never had Robin. And Robin represented the best part of her life.

"We all make mistakes," he muttered, shutting his toolbox and snapping the lock into place. He wanted no part of her personal life. The less he knew, the more distant he could remain. "Yours was not getting this van serviced on a regular basis."

Her mouth curved again. This time, he noticed that the amusement didn't reach her eyes. "I had what you might call a cash-flow problem. I earned the cash, and it would flow right through Jim's hands."

"A gambler," Malcolm guessed, putting two and two together.

Christa raised her voice to be heard above the thud of his toolbox landing on the floorboards. "With a capital *G*."

Malcolm shut the door. He was getting ready to leave, she thought. She wanted him to remain at least for a little while. Though he was uncommunicative, there was something comforting about having him around. She liked talking to him.

"That's how I knew who you were," she said.

Malcolm raised his eyes to her face sharply.

"Oh, not at first," she explained quickly, "not even after your brilliant display of driving skills. Not even after I saw you," she admitted. "It was your name."

"My name?" His success had earned him some notoriety, but nothing on a large scale.

She nodded. "On the sign at your garage. Jim bet on you once. The big race at Laguna. You made him rich." She remembered the excitement. Jim had been so sure his luck had finally changed. "For a week or so."

Malcolm recalled the race. It was the last one he entered. "He bet on me?"

Christa laughed lightly at the surprise she detected in his voice. He wouldn't have been surprised if he had known her husband.

"Jim bet on everything and anything." Her expression sobered slightly. "Except our marriage. That, he just gambled on. And lost.

"Hungry?" she asked brightly, changing topics as sharply and cleanly as he changed lanes during practice.

"No," he lied.

His belly was empty, but he had gotten accustomed to that sort of feeling. It was the other emptiness that he couldn't find a way to deal with.

Christa refused to believe him. "You have to be," she insisted, brooking no argument. "And I've got a meal that can be eaten hot or cold." She'd made fried chicken, prepared for all contingencies and any excuse. She raised her eyes hopefully to his face. "Please?"

He should have said no, he thought as he followed her inside. He really should have.

But the warm glow coming from the open door beckoned to him. It was too much to resist.

Chapter Five

It definitely wasn't what he'd expected.

If Malcolm had stopped to try to envision the type of house someone like Christa would live in, he would have placed her in one filled with knickknacks that were overflowing from strategically placed tables and shelves.

Instead, the house was as barren as the site of a freshly perpetrated major burglary.

There was not a sofa or recliner in the tiny living room. Rather, there were three lawn chairs, all mismatched. They were arranged around a coffee table that appeared to be listing to one side. The only thing that looked to be even mildly new was the small TV set, and it was actually standing on an orange crate.

Christa glanced at Malcolm as she led the way to the kitchen, curious about his reaction. His expression was impassive, but there was a hint of surprise in his eyes—as well there should be, she mused. The furnishings were Spartan even by a monk's standards.

He could feel her looking at him and knew she was probably waiting for him to comment.

"Eclectic," he murmured.

Well, at least he was polite. It touched her.

"Borrowed," she corrected.

The kitchen had a far sturdier table, freshly removed from her father's garage, where it had previously been used to accommodate old newspapers. The four chairs surrounding it were of the folding variety, compliments of her other brother, Ethan. Weekly poker games at his house had been temporarily adjourned to another location.

She gestured Malcolm to one of the chairs as she opened the small refrigerator.

"There wasn't exactly money to burn when I left Jim," she said, answering the silent question she was certain was crossing his mind. "We lived in a furnished apartment. He didn't want to 'waste money' on anything he couldn't hock." And she had gone along with that, at least for a while. It still amazed her what a person could overlook in the name of love.

"The dining room—" she nodded at the tiny alcove they'd passed "—doesn't have a table yet. We'll eat here," she added needlessly. Taking out the platter of fried chicken she'd prepared earlier, she placed it in the middle of the table. Her mouth quirked in the slightly slanted smile he was beginning to anticipate as she took out two plates, one for each of them. "At least this table doesn't take a bow every time you put something on it." Taking a seat opposite Malcolm, she nodded toward the living room. "Ethan's old coffee table does tricks."

It had collapsed under the weight of the *TV Guide* yesterday. Wood glue and a folded playing card under one of the legs temporarily remedied the situation.

Christa couldn't wait to buy real furniture again. But that might not be anytime soon.

"Ethan?"

She moved a napkin beside the plates. "My other brother. He's a cop, too." Ethan had been the last to join the force, following his heart rather than his now-ex-wife's protests. A motorcycle policeman with the highway patrol, he claimed his work made him happier than his ex-wife had. "Like my dad was before him."

Malcolm wondered how a gambler had managed to infiltrate a house full of policemen long enough to whisk her away, and then told himself he wasn't interested. Not his business what she did or why. It occurred to him that it wasn't the first time he had thought that, and each time, his conviction had slipped a half notch.

The pause in conversation felt uncomfortable. Malcolm nodded vaguely at the information she offered. "Must make you feel safe."

She laughed. She'd never really thought about it, except perhaps in terms of rebellion. She'd had three authority figures to pit herself against instead of just one. Her mother, bless her, had always been on her side, even when, Christa suspected, the older woman had known she was wrong.

"Still didn't keep me from making mistakes," Christa mused out loud.

Their eyes met for a moment. He was getting in too close again. Malcolm placed his hands against the table, ready to push himself away. He felt no resistance and decided that perhaps pushing the table wouldn't be the wisest thing.

Neither was coming inside the condo.

"It's late. I really should be going."

There was something in his manner that told her he didn't want to leave, even if he said so. Without thinking, she laid her hand over his.

"At least let me repay one kindness with another." Laughter entered her eyes.

Funny how easily and frequently that seemed to happen, he thought, especially under the circumstances.

"Although," she continued, "you might not think so after you have some of my chicken." She'd never developed her mother's knack for cooking. Or her father's, for that matter. "You probably fix cars a lot better than I can cook."

Another woman would have snowed him with her culinary abilities to make him stay. Christa won him over with her honesty. Relenting, Malcolm reached for a piece of chicken.

"You don't exactly build a winning argument for yourself, do you?"

A small feeling of triumph budded within her. "Oh, I don't know. Now you feel bound to stay and sample, just to make me feel better."

Malcolm shook his head before bothering to take a bite. "Maybe I was wrong."

She cocked her head, looking, he thought, incredibly like her daughter had just before she'd patted his face. There was something innocently captivating about both of them.

"About what?"

"About you being calculating." He took a bite and then another.

The single approving nod made satisfaction flower and spread within her.

She raised her hands in surrender. "Ah, well, you found me out. After living with a gambler for five years,

figuring out odds and angles just becomes second nature
to you.''

As did unfounded hope, she added silently. Except hers
was always centered around people, not on the turn of a
card or the spin of a wheel.

The fried chicken legs were small. He reached for another, their tangy flavor wrapping around his taste buds
and urging him on. He'd had only a fast-food ham-
burger for lunch. And enough coffee to float a battle-
ship.

His thoughts reverted to the woman sitting opposite
him. ''Did you gamble, too?''

She shook her head adamantly. Watching Jim destroy
himself had been lesson enough for her, not that she had
ever been inclined to pit herself against Lady Luck. ''Not
even at Monopoly.''

He raised his eyes to her face. Her mouth was curved,
but she was deadly serious. *Must have been burned bad,*
he decided.

She didn't want to talk about the negative part of her
life. She wanted to learn something about him.

''Enough about me.'' Toying with the remainder of the
chicken breast on her own plate, Christa looked at him.
Her curiosity was almost tangible. ''Let's talk about
you.''

His eyes remained on his plate as he slowly wiped his
fingers. ''Let's not.''

It was a softly issued order, but she blatantly ignored
it as if it had never been uttered. ''You were a racer,'' she
began.

They had already established that. ''Yes.''

She knew next to nothing about the world of sports,
except that it had afforded Jim yet another avenue in

which to lose his money. "Were you any good at it? Besides the Laguna race, I mean?"

The simplicity of her question amused him. It was obvious that she had never followed the sport, which was just as well. The last thing he needed was a nostalgic groupie. He had shaken off more than his share during the ten years he'd raced.

He shrugged. "A fair amount of success." It had been a hell of a lot more than that, but he didn't see the need or the purpose to mention it. It had never been in his nature to brag, and besides, it was all old ground now. As far behind him as if it had never happened.

She didn't understand. Doing something for a living that you loved and were good at was the ultimate dream come true. "If you were good at it, why did you stop?"

He avoided her eyes. He definitely wasn't going to go into that. "Reflexes got slow."

He was lying to her. There was another reason. She crossed the line of polite hostess and entered dangerous ground as she probed. "Not the way Tyler told me you were driving today. You obviously love cars—"

"And you obviously love asking questions," he said, cutting her off, the smile on his lips cold, without feeling.

She conceded the point easily. "Yes, I do. It's the only way to learn about people."

He pushed back his plate, his eyes challenging her, warning her that it was dangerous to continue. "What if they don't want to be learned about? What if they want things to be kept private?"

She knew what he was saying. But something deep within her told her that he was lonely. That he needed a friend as much as she had needed one once. Maybe more.

"I don't gossip, if that's what you mean," she told him quietly. Christa leaned forward, her eyes kind, intense. "I'd like to be friends."

Malcolm leaned away from her, away from the hand she was figuratively offering him. "I have enough friends. You are a customer."

The rebuff was almost physical. It took her a moment to recover.

Christa blew out a long breath as she shook her head to clear it. "Well, that certainly puts me in my place, doesn't it?"

It was a quip, but there was hurt in her eyes. Something akin to guilt burrowed through him, pushing its way forward. It was her own fault, damn it. "I didn't mean—"

Her smile was quick, bathing him in redemption. He realized that he didn't begin to understand her.

"Yes, you did, but that's okay. Fortunately for you, I have a hide like a rhino." Avoiding his eyes, she urged another piece of chicken onto his plate. Her own remained bare, save for the bones of the one breast. "That's a prerequisite to having lived the kind of life I've lived. Reflexes aren't necessary, tough skin is." Her smile was a little tight, but she worked on it.

Christa rose. "Can I offer you something to drink?" She reached for two glasses in the cupboard before he answered.

Tough skin or not, he'd hurt her feelings and he hadn't really meant to. He had just wanted her to back off. He didn't talk about himself or what had made him forever turn his back on racing. Not with any of the people he had once called friends and certainly not with a stranger. Even an appealing one who had a tendency to ramble.

Still, he hadn't wanted to hurt her. From what she had told him, it sounded as if she'd gone through enough as it was.

"A cola if you have it. Water if you don't."

"As luck would have it, I have a couple of cans of diet cola left."

She bent over, searching for one of them in the refrigerator. He allowed himself a moment to admire the view before she straightened. Legs like that didn't happen except in a man's fantasy, he thought.

Their eyes met again. There was amusement in hers.

Malcolm looked for something to say. "What made you come back here?"

That was an easy one. "My family was here. We'd all grown up in Bedford—my brothers and I," she clarified. "I can remember when this was a three-traffic-light city and the main thoroughfare was a two-lane road." Nostalgia flitted over her face. "It was the happiest time of my life."

And she wished she could go back. Her father had run a strict household, but there was never any question that they were all loved, all secure. She'd never known about insecurity until she had married Jim. Then nothing was secure *except* insecurity.

Popping the tab on the can of soda, she placed it in front of him. "You?"

He thought of the conscious choice he'd made after a great deal of looking around and reading. He'd become satisfied that Bedford was the best place to raise Sally, a good, clean city where crime meant carelessly dropping a gum wrapper on the street and the school system was one of the best in the country.

"Just someplace I drifted to."

He didn't strike her as the type to drift. Unless there was a reason to make him.

"After your wife died?" The sharp look in his eyes simultaneously warned her off and told her she had guessed right.

It was simpler to lie. "Yes." He was talking too much, he admonished himself. Saying things he had no intention of saying or sharing.

She wanted to reach him, she thought, to soothe him. Not because he had saved her child, not because he was an exceptionally good looking man, but because he was hurting. And she knew what it meant to hurt and not know how to heal.

"So there are no memories here for you," she concluded softly.

"No." None that he would allow himself to remember.

"Me, I came back for the memories. Memories of happier times," she confided readily.

She had had to swallow her pride to do it, but her family had been remarkable and rallied around her. No one said, *I told you so.* What they had said was, *How can I help?* It was all she could do to keep Tyler and Ethan from coming and getting her. But she had been determined to return on her own. And to make it work as best as possible.

"I intend to build on that. The happiness. To have Robin grow up in a place where I was happy." A nostalgic smile played on her lips. "I thought it might rub off on both of us."

"You don't seem to be having much trouble being happy." Not from what he'd witnessed so far.

Christa grinned. "I have an annoyingly bouncy-perky nature." That's what Jim had accused her of in one of his blacker moods.

Malcolm wondered if she was second-guessing his own reaction to her. "I wouldn't say annoying."

Amusement lit up her face. "All right, what would you say?"

He paused, searching for the right word. He settled rather than chose. Words had never been his medium. "Persistent."

His answer delighted her. "I didn't know you were a diplomat, too."

There was something about just sitting here, talking to her in her sparse kitchen, that coaxed a smile from him. He decided that perhaps she was infectious.

"You learn to be a lot of things when you have to tell a man it's going to cost over a thousand dollars to fix his car."

For a moment, talking to him, she'd forgotten about the cold, hard reality sitting out in her driveway. She remembered now. Christa blew out a breath, then pressed her lips together, bracing herself.

"And how much is it going to cost to fix mine?"

Too much. But he didn't want to spoil her evening. He would see what kind of corners he could cut for her through his various connections with discount suppliers. But he didn't want to raise her hopes, either.

He remained closemouthed. "I haven't come up with an estimate yet."

She'd learned how to interpret evasions. "That bad, huh?"

Well, there was some hope for her. She wasn't a complete optimist.

Malcolm avoided answering the question directly. "Your car needs a lot of work."

She looked around the room. The long, narrow kitchen was empty except for the table and chairs and the small, combination refrigerator-stove she'd purchased at a secondhand store. The rest of the house, save for Robin's room, was similarly unfurnished, and the walls could stand to be painted.

"Everything in my life needs work." Her smile became affectionate. "Except for Robin."

As if her daughter had been waiting to be mentioned, a mournful wail emerged, floating down from the second floor.

Christa rose quickly. "Excuse me, that would be my cue." Before leaving, she pushed the platter of chicken closer to his plate. "Keep eating. You couldn't possibly be satisfied with such a tiny serving."

He would have said that about life once, he thought as she left. But as it turned out, all he had wanted out of life *was* one tiny serving.

A tiny serving of happiness, wrapped around his wife and daughter.

Robin's wail became more insistent, more frightened. Christa hurried up the winding staircase. Robin's bedroom was only half a landing away. The condo was staggered so that three floors were wedged into a structure where normally there might be two; each had its own narrow hall and half bath.

"Mommy's coming, honey. Mommy's coming," Christa called out reassuringly.

Robin was having another one of her nightmares. Last night had been the first time she had slept straight through. Christa had hoped it was the beginning of a pattern. Or rather, an end to one.

Robin was sitting up in her bed, holding on to the side railing with tight, sweaty fingers. The room, unlike the others in the house, was completely furnished. There was a lamp on, not just a night-light, to hold back the night and the scary things the darkness created just by being dark.

The lamp, the bed and the tiny table and chairs, not to mention the brimming toy chest, had all made the trip over the desert with them. Christa had purposely surrounded her daughter with all the familiar things from her room in Las Vegas. She'd hoped to make the transition easier for Robin.

Robin had been the ultimate reason she'd made the move in the first place.

"Dleem," Robin sobbed, holding her hands out to her mother.

"I know, honey, I know." Christa picked her up, holding her close. "It was that bad dream again, wasn't it?"

In reply, Robin buried her head against Christa's shoulder and sobbed.

"Shh, it's over, honey." She swayed to and fro, hoping the motion would soothe Robin. "All over. Nothing to be afraid of."

"Maybe she was dreaming about the car-jacking."

Christa started, surprised that Malcolm had followed her up. She would have thought he'd be relieved not to be dragged upstairs with her.

She nodded as she stroked the silky blond head resting against her shoulder.

"She's been having nightmares for a while now." A rueful smile curved her mouth. "I think it has to do with waking up one night and hearing Jim and me arguing." She might as well call a spade a spade. "Shouting, actually. It frightened her pretty badly.'' She looked at him over her daughter's head. "That was when I knew I had to get out. Before it scarred her.'' She flushed. "I guess I didn't go fast enough.''

Without thinking, Malcolm stroked the tiny head. "Maybe it's not your fault. Maybe she's just having a dream about there not being enough chocolate ice cream in the world.''

Christa looked at him, bemused, but he was being serious. And his attention was completely focused on Robin. There was a softer look in his eyes than she had seen so far this evening. Because it seemed somehow natural, she moved the child toward him.

He offered no protest as he took Robin into his arms. Malcolm looked down at the tearstained face. The tiny tear tracks were beginning to dry. "Bad dream, Robin?''

The girl sniffled and shoved her thumb deep into her mouth as she nodded in reply.

Remembering what Malcolm had told her about the end result of thumb sucking, Christa began to remove the thumb from Robin's mouth. Robin wiggled farther into Malcolm's chest. "Don't, honey.''

Malcolm moved her hand away from the little girl, still looking at Robin. "That's okay,'' he murmured.

Christa stared at him, bemused. "You were the one who pointed out the future ortho bills.''

"One more time won't hurt.'' The rule was for the daytime, when there weren't things that went bump in the dark. "It makes her feel better.'' He resisted the temptation to kiss the silken head, the way he'd done countless times with his own daughter. "Doesn't it, Robin?''

She murmured, making a noise he took to mean yes. The warm breath against his chest evoked a thousand memories in his mind, all bittersweet. They traveled through him like spun sugar, breaking so that there were sharp, jagged edges everywhere. Edges that pricked him and made him bleed.

He had a daughter of his own, Christa thought suddenly. Or had.

Where was that child now?

Malcolm looked down at Robin. He couldn't see her face, but he felt the even breathing. "I think she's asleep," he told Christa.

"Just like that?" It usually took her more than half an hour of walking the floor before Robin was calm enough to fall back asleep.

"Just like that," he whispered.

Edging Christa away with his elbow, he laid Robin back into the bed. Christa pulled the light sheet over the small form, then tiptoed after the man who was a total enigma to her.

"You know, you're wasting your time as a mechanic," she whispered to him outside of Robin's door. "You should be hiring out as a miracle worker."

She had made him smile again. "I thought that was what mechanics were supposed to be." Then his smile faded again as he became aware of her, of the heat of her body wafting to his.

He was standing too close to her. Too close to feelings he didn't want.

Malcolm took a step toward the stairs. "I'd better go."

They hadn't really finished eating yet. And she had a dessert planned. "The chicken—"

"Was very good, but I've got an early morning."

He'd made up his mind. She couldn't very well throw a rope over him and tie him down. Christa nodded as she shoved a hand into her front pocket. Her finger came in contact with the button she'd picked up earlier.

"Your shirt," she said, suddenly remembering. She reached out and touched the empty buttonhole. "I promised to sew it."

His hand covered hers. He meant to move it aside. Somehow, his hand remained there. The contact warmed him more than it should have. "I can handle that."

What he couldn't handle, he thought, was his reaction to her, to the little girl and to being here in general. It all felt too good and it shouldn't. It shouldn't have ever felt good again.

Her laugh was light, like her daughter's. "Well, you've convinced me that you can handle just about anything. My car, my daughter. My cooking." She thought back to what he had said at the table. "Some of my interrogation."

Self-conscious, he let his hand drop to his side. "I didn't mean what I said earlier."

Christa turned her face up to his. The light from Robin's room played on the delicate outline, softening it even more.

Making it tempting. When was the last time he'd been remotely tempted? He couldn't remember.

"Already forgotten," she told him.

But what wasn't forgotten, there in the narrow, dim hallway, was the fact that he was a man and he was hurting. And maybe he was not quite as strong as he thought he was or wanted to be.

The brush of her body against his as she moved forward sent waves of something basic and unmanageable through him. Before he could think or hold himself in check, Malcolm reacted.

His hand cupping the long, slender column of her throat, he stroked his thumb along her pulse point. It jumped and echoed his own.

Malcolm brought his mouth down to hers.

And shot his successful, uncontested retreat all to hell.

Chapter Six

Like a contestant in a game show who had selected a secret door, Malcolm thought he had a vague idea of what was in store for him.

Two seconds after he'd made his choice to kiss Christa, he discovered that he hadn't had a clue.

What he expected, hoped, was that perhaps the kiss would somehow ease the ache he felt a little. Not the one in his heart, but the one in his gut. The one she had caused. Perhaps he even expected the sweetness.

But not to this degree, and he certainly hadn't expected that sweetness to both soothe and agitate the ache within him.

It made him want more. A great deal more.

Wanting was a sensation he'd almost forgotten. To want a woman, to want to hold her and make love with her. To bury his face in her hair and breathe in the soft, delicate fragrance he found there. To turn in the stillness of the night and find someone beside him, breathing evenly, lost in sleep.

All these longings seemed like relics from another time, when he'd felt whole. When he had felt *anything*. Suddenly, he wanted these things back in his life with a passion that stunned him.

Drawing Christa closer into his arms, Malcolm fed on the sustenance she offered. The kiss deepened so that it took on the aspect of a chasm.

The danger with chasms was that people occasionally fell into them.

And he did.

The sparks came quickly and then took over everything. Christa didn't realize that she had dug her fingers into his shoulders until she felt them cramping. Whether she was holding on for support or pulling him toward her she wouldn't have been able to say even under oath. All she knew was that this feeling vibrating through her was something very, very new.

She heard a moan, and it surprised her that the sound was coming from her. She wasn't the type to moan. Love for her had been an easy, friendly thing. Never before had she experienced the sensation of being bodily tossed about in a tumultuous sea.

She did now.

Christa had been content in what she deemed was adult love. She'd certainly never craved passion. Yet here she was, sopping it up like a dry, insatiable sponge.

Her fingers tangled in his hair as her body leaned into his, drawn by a force she couldn't resist.

Didn't want to resist.

If her body felt any hotter, she was sure it would ignite on its own, exploding like a Fourth of July sparkler.

She'd always liked the Fourth of July.

There was absolutely no air left in her lungs when Malcolm drew away. She couldn't have mustered enough breath to blow out a single candle if she tried. Christa felt emotionally spent. One moment, he was leaving; the next, he was reducing her to cinders.

Had she missed something here?

Trying to discreetly draw in enough oxygen to function, Christa needed more than a moment to orient herself.

She looked at Malcolm in unabashed wonder. "You liked the chicken that much?"

He didn't realize he was laughing until he heard the deep, rumbling sound resonating in his ears. The amazement in her eyes tickled him in a way he hadn't experienced in years. God, but it felt good to laugh, really laugh again.

"Yes, I liked the chicken that much."

Christa nodded her head without realizing it. She was still trying to get her pulse to unscramble and her brain to engage.

So this was what they meant by being knocked off your feet.

"Maybe I should start a franchise." And then she smiled at him, the expression blooming in her eyes.

He could see it, even in the dim light. Somehow, the smile filtered into his chest and branded him. He didn't think to resist. "That would certainly beat going in for the interview tomorrow."

She'd almost forgotten about the interview. It didn't loom before her like a foreboding entity any longer. Not after she'd been knocked over like a lone pin in a bowling alley during a hurricane.

Because they couldn't remain standing there indefinitely, Christa took the initiative. She turned and walked down the stairs to the first floor.

Malcolm watched the slight sway of her hips as she walked and told himself not to. "What is it that you do, anyway?"

It took her a minute to remember that, too. "I'm an accountant." She turned to look at him. His eyes were dark again, and he was growing distant. Had that really been him on the landing? "So was Jim until he thought he discovered the perfect system to beat the odds."

Malcolm thought of fate and the accident. "Nobody can beat the odds."

She pressed her lips together and tasted him. Tasted the desire, his and her own, and was surprised by both.

"Oh, I don't know." Her eyes searched his, looking for a clue to the man who was hidden from her. "Sometimes you can."

He didn't have to be told that she wasn't talking about the gambling tables in Las Vegas. She was talking about something far more personal. And he didn't want to go into it. He'd made enough mistakes for one evening.

He had to leave while he could still reasonably function. The tiny ray of sunshine she'd created within him was now being blocked out by a cloud of guilt that was growing to giant proportions.

Guilt that had its tentacles wrapped up in the past. He had no business feeling this way about another woman, not when if he'd been just a little quicker, a little sharper, Gloria would have been standing here beside him. Alive.

And he wouldn't have felt so dead inside.

Malcolm walked into the living room. He looked around mechanically. On second thought, the small room with its improbable furniture seemed to suit her after all.

Malcolm shoved his hands into his back pockets and turned, only to find Christa directly behind him. In her defense, there wasn't that much room for her to utilize. But even if there had been the length of a football stadium between them, somehow it would have still felt too close.

"What do you plan to do about the interview?"

She sighed, thinking. As much as she wanted to savor what had just happened, tomorrow would be here soon enough, and with it, more bills.

Christa lifted her shoulders in a resigned shrug. As she saw it, there was only one option open to her. "I need a job and as quickly as possible. I figure I'll call a cab."

Wasn't there anyone else she could call? "Cabs cost money."

Everything cost money. Except friendship, she mused. And whether he realized it or not, they were well on their way to forming one.

Her grin was like quicksilver. "Tell me something I don't know."

He shouldn't be standing here telling her anything. He should have been home hours ago. Nodding vaguely at her comment, he walked to the front door.

When he opened it, he turned to bid her good-night, then stopped. How could such a small woman have such a large impact? Or had he just imagined what had happened outside her daughter's room?

"Thanks for the chicken."

Christa rested her head against the door. "Don't mention it. It's me who should be thanking you for everything else."

"Yeah, well..." His voice trailed off as he began to leave. Abruptly, he stopped without turning around. He was going to regret this. The words came anyway. "About the cab tomorrow."

"Yes?"

He still didn't turn around. Somehow, it was easier to make the offer without seeing the look in her eyes. "Don't call it."

She didn't understand. Was he telling her not to go to the interview? But why?

"I have to in order to get to the interview." Christa had no means of transportation available to her, not with the van sitting like a gutted Buddha in her driveway. "And I already mentioned that my father won't lend out his—"

"I'll drive you."

Maybe she hadn't heard him correctly. "Excuse me?"

"I'll drive you," he repeated, biting off each word as if it were made of hard licorice. He had no fondness for licorice.

Maybe that kiss *had* rattled her brain. "*You'll* drive me?"

This time, he did turn around. When he did, there was a trace of annoyance creasing his brow. Christa had the impression that he was more annoyed with himself than with her.

"I just said that, didn't I?"

The smile on her lips spread, taking over her entire face and growing wider with each word she uttered. "Yes, you did."

He wished she wouldn't look at him like that, as if he was some sort of a savior. He was nobody's savior. But he couldn't very well leave her stranded. Never mind that she wasn't his responsibility.

"So what time is it? The interview," he added when she didn't answer him immediately.

"Ten."

"Ten," he repeated. "Far?"

"Newport Center Drive, just on the outskirts of Fashion Island." She named the popular outdoor mall.

"I'll be here tomorrow morning at nine-thirty."

With those words hanging in the air between them, he left. He didn't wait for her to thank him or to even say good-night.

Christa stood in the doorway, watching him leave, a bemused smile on her lips. She waved in case he turned around again. He didn't.

Someday, she thought, running her fingers over her mouth, he would.

He had to be the most reluctant Good Samaritan ever created, she mused.

Things were going to turn out just fine. Christa closed the door behind her and began to hum. She hummed for a very long time.

At exactly 9:20 a.m., Malcolm arrived at her doorstep. He noted absently that the Jaguar wasn't parked where it had been yesterday and wondered if her father lived close by and had decided to walk.

He was getting entirely too wrapped up in her day-to-day life, he upbraided himself, ringing the doorbell.

Christa answered immediately. Dressed in a teal blue suit that would have made a man notice her in a crowd of hundreds, she offered him a rueful smile.

"I'm afraid you came for nothing," she apologized. "You can go on to work. I'm sorry I imposed on you."

Her words were sending him away, but she held the door open wide, silently inviting him in. He chose neutral ground and remained on the doorstep.

It was a little late for apologies in his book. "They canceled the interview?"

"No, but I'm going to have to cancel it. My father can't make it."

He nodded at her suit. "You're still dressed for the interview."

"That's because he just called me. He slept late," she explained. The details had come out garbled, and she was still trying to sort them out. "As near as I can make out, my father's date wanted to go out for sushi, and it apparently didn't agree with him. He's home sick, and I can't get a sitter on ten minutes' notice. The only good thing that's come out of this is that his date feels so guilty, she's coming by later to take care of him." She smiled, though for the life of him, Malcolm couldn't see why. "They really hit it off."

The interview was important to her. How could she be happy at a time like this? He didn't understand. He also didn't understand what he was still doing here. He'd done the polite thing, the more than polite thing. He'd made an offer and tried to live up to it. It wasn't his fault that her father had canceled at the last minute. His conscience was more than appeased and completely in the clear.

All he had to do was turn around and leave.

There was absolutely no earthly reason for him to do what he did next. Damning himself for being an idiot, he dug into the front pocket of his jeans.

"Here."

Christa looked down at the set of keys he had handed her. There was a tiny silver race car attached to the chain. She wondered if his wife had given it to him. "Here, what?"

Was she blind? "Here are my keys."

She closed her hand over them, still confused. "I know they're keys," she answered patiently, "but why are you handing them to me?" She would have thought that he would be even more possessive of his car than her father was of his.

Malcolm thought his offer would have been obvious to her. "Because you can't drive the car without them." She was still staring at him, dumbfounded, so he added, "I'm telling you to drive yourself over to the interview. I'll stay here with Robin."

She could understand his offering to fix her car. It was what he did. Staying with a small, overenergetic child was not part of his job description. "Let me get this straight—you're offering to baby-sit my daughter?"

She was making this worse. He shrugged self-consciously. "It's not that big a deal. I didn't offer to adopt her, I just said I'd stay with her for a little while." The frown on his face deepened, as if he was checking the situation for loopholes. "They're not planning to ask you out to lunch or anything, are they?"

She shook her head. "No, this is strictly just an office interview." She glanced over her shoulder at Robin. The little girl was planted on the floor in front of the TV set, watching a huge yellow bird lead the neighborhood children on a scavenger hunt for the letter *B*. "I don't know what to say."

The last thing he wanted was for her to launch into a speech about how grateful she was. "Don't say anything. Please," he added for good measure. Malcolm glanced at his watch impatiently. "You're going to be late if you don't leave soon."

He was right, absolutely right. "Yes, I am. Thanks."

Christa hesitated in the doorway. It was better all around if she didn't say goodbye to Robin. She'd learned by experience that Robin didn't do well with leave-taking, but if she found someone else in her mother's stead, that seemed to be all right.

Picking up her purse, Christa began to leave, then quickly retraced her steps. Her father was already familiar with the routine, but Malcolm wasn't.

Malcolm looked at her, his impatience mounting. "What?"

Christa gestured at Robin, who was still oblivious to them. "She's been fed and changed, and all you have to do is watch TV with her."

"I know how to take care of a two-year-old. Now get going." With that, he almost pushed her out the front door.

"Yes, of course." Holding on to his arm, she brushed a quick kiss on his lips and then hurried down the driveway to his car.

He had to be crazy to be doing this, Malcolm thought. But he'd already made arrangements with Jock, calling the teenager late last night and telling him that he was going to be taking the morning off. Seemed a shame to let her miss her interview since he'd made himself available this way.

She'd probably crash the LeMans, he thought darkly as he watched her climb into his car. He was just about to close the door when he saw her climb out again.

"Now what?" he called out to her.

Maybe the job just wasn't meant to happen for her, Christa thought as she walked back into the condo. "It's a stick shift."

He didn't see the problem. "I know it's a stick shift. So?"

"I don't know how to drive one." The thought of stepping on the clutch every time she had to change gears was completely overwhelming to her. "It's too much like tap dancing."

A stick shift was the only way to really feel as if you were in control of the car, but he figured the point would be lost on Christa. Malcolm sighed. Now wasn't the time to give her a quick lesson. Her father wasn't the only one who valued his car, and besides, the interview was in half an hour. He was ready to say "Forget it," but the look in her eyes stopped him.

Damn it all to hell, anyway.

Malcolm didn't bother thinking it through. "All right, I'll drive you."

"But I can't leave Robin and I can't very well go in with her, either."

"Don't you think I already know that?" he said tersely. "We'll take her with us, and I'll watch her while you have your interview." He looked around, remembering the huge diaper bag Gloria had always lugged around. "Does she have any stuff we have to take with us?"

Hope reappeared. "Yes, she has 'stuff.'"

"Then get it together."

"It already is." Experience had taught her to keep a fully packed diaper bag handy in case of emergencies. Picking up at a moment's notice had been something she had learned how to do during her marriage.

Taking the bag from the floor in the closet, Christa patted it on the side. "Everything we need is in here."

Malcolm glanced at it as he went to pick up Robin. He didn't notice the pleased look on Christa's face as he took the little girl into his arms.

"I doubt it." Without waiting for her, he led the way out. "It doesn't look big enough for a shrink."

Christa hurriedly turned off the TV set and followed them out of the house. "Why would I need a shrink?" She locked the door behind her.

"Not you, me." He turned around to look at her. "Someone to examine my head."

She waved a hand at his words. "Your head's just fine. And your heart's a lot bigger than I thought it would be." And if hearing her say it bothered him, too bad. It was true.

Setting the diaper bag down beside her van, Christa struggled to pry the car seat out.

Illogical woman, never going about anything the right way. "Here," he said, handing her Robin. As she took her daughter, he moved them both out of the way. "You hold on to your daughter, I'll get the car seat."

"Whatever you want." Christa feigned meekness.

"Yeah, right," Malcolm muttered under his breath.

Christa just stood back and smiled.

They'd made excellent time. Traffic at nine-thirty was light and moving. Robin was making some sort of noise behind them.

Probably thought she was singing along with the radio, he mused. He glanced at Christa, who had remained rather quiet, given her personality. He could only attribute it to one thing.

"Nervous?"

She had long since grown past having butterflies. "I've been running around too much this morning to think about being nervous."

Her words struck a familiar chord. "Yeah, I know how that is." He made a right off MacArthur. The outdoor mall and its outlining office buildings lay just beyond the traffic light.

She watched him shift, fascinated that he did it with such ease, without even appearing to think about it. If it were her, she would still be trying to get out of the cul-de-sac. "Is that what you did before a race? Kept busy so that you wouldn't think about it?"

He thought about it, all right, but only in terms of the finish line, never in terms of what might be waiting for him along the hairpin turns he took around the track.

"There was always so much to check, to go over." His mouth curved slightly as he remembered. "Somehow, the race itself just happened while I was mentally reviewing checklists."

She liked the way his face softened when he talked about his racing days. "How long were you in it?"

He knew that down to the second, but there was no need to mention it. "Ten years—officially."

That was an odd way to put it. Did racers apprentice? "And unofficially?"

He ran his hand over the steering wheel as he made a left. Office buildings flanked the street on either side, while the mall beckoned in front of him. "I've been driving since I was twelve."

That was impossible, yet he didn't seem like the type to brag. "Twelve?"

He heard the skepticism in her voice. "Tractors," he clarified.

"You're a farm boy?" She tried to picture him on a farm and couldn't.

"I was." It hadn't been a happy time for him. He'd only been marking time until the day he could get away. Now he was just marking time.

"Do you miss it?"

He offered her another glance. "If I did, I'd be back there."

Yes, he would, she thought. Malcolm wasn't the type to just let life take him along to places he didn't want to go.

"Speaking of being there, we are." She gestured toward the building he had almost passed. It was just short of the mall.

Malcolm made a sharp right, pulling into the parking lot. As they entered, she could feel the butterflies beginning to get ready for takeoff. Maybe she wasn't home free after all.

She concentrated on Robin and not on how important this was to her. Getting out, Christa quickly unfastened the buckles around the little girl. Giving her one last hug, Christa passed Robin to Malcolm.

"I think you'll find everything you need in there." She nodded at the oversize bag and then flushed, realizing she'd already told him that. "I'll try to be as quick as I can," she promised.

He nodded curtly. "Just get the job so that this is worth it."

His words didn't match his deeds. She had perhaps five minutes to spare and paused, looking at him. There were no answers in his eyes, only reasons for her to have more questions.

"Why are you doing this? Coming to my rescue all the time?"

He didn't like being questioned. Holding Robin, he slung the bag over his shoulder. "Penance."

She had a feeling he wasn't being flippant. For now, she let it go. But there would be other times, she promised herself silently.

Uncertainty nibbled at her. "Sure you'll be all right while I'm here?"

"Don't worry about it," he told her. "I'll take her to the mall. They've built it up some in the last few years. Should be something there to entertain her while you're gone." He was already walking away. "I'll meet you back here in an hour."

She nodded, bracing her shoulders. The firm she was interviewing with was on the fourth floor. If she got the job, she'd probably be able to see all the way to Catalina on a clear day. The thought heartened her. Almost as much as seeing the way Robin had taken to Malcolm.

That made two of them, she mused.

"Well, here goes nothing."

"Everything," he corrected deliberately. "Here goes everything."

She nodded, hand on the door. "Right."

There weren't too many people frequenting the outdoor mall on a weekday morning. Malcolm had most of the area to himself, which was just as well. He didn't care for crowds and noise anymore. Not the way he had once.

Outdoor vendors eyed him hopefully as he walked with Robin in his arms. He'd tried walking hand in hand with her, but it took five of her childish steps to match one of his and he'd begun to develop a crick in his neck. Holding her in his arms was easier, at least on his neck.

His heart was another matter.

He looked at the tiny, expressive face. She looked a lot like her mother, he realized. "So, what do you want to do while we wait?"

There was no hesitancy in her answer. "See Bibur."

"Bibur?" What the hell was Bibur? Above them, the wind whipped the edges of a small shop's yellow awning. The color connected with an image. He remem-

Dear Reader,

YOU MAY BE A MAILBOX AWAY FROM BEING OUR NEW MILLION $$ WINNER!

Scratch off the gold on Game Cards 1-7 to automatically qualify for a chance to win a cash prize of up to $1 Million in lifetime cash! Do the same on Game Cards 8 & 9 to automatically get free books and a free surprise gift -- and to try Silhouette's no-risk Reader Service. It's a delightful way to get our best novels each month -- at discount -- with no obligation to buy, ever. Here's how it works, satisfaction fully guaranteed:

After receiving your free books, if you don't want any more, just write "cancel" on the accompanying statement, and return it to us. If you do not cancel, each month we'll send you 6 additional novels to read and enjoy & bill you just $2.67 each plus 25¢ delivery and applicable sales tax, if any.* That's the complete price, and -- compared to cover prices of $3.25 each -- quite a bargain!

You may cancel at any time, but if you choose to continue, every month we'll send you 6 more books, which you may either purchase at the discount price...or return to us and cancel your subscription.

P.S. Don't Forget to include your Bonus Token.

SEE BACK OF BOOK FOR SWEEPSTAKES DETAILS. ENTER TODAY, AND... *Good Luck!*

▲ CAREFULLY PRE-FOLD & TEAR ALONG DOTTED LINES, MOISTEN & FOLD OVER FLAP TO SEAL REPLY ▼

bered the program she'd been watching just before they left. "Big Bird?" he asked.

Her face was a wreath of smiles. "Bibur."

"Sorry, he's probably in New York."

Malcolm looked around. They had really remodeled the mall since he had been here last. Nothing was where it was supposed to be. Everything seemed to be centered around a huge fountain that periodically shot up water. A myriad of stores, arranged along six different paths that all led to the fountain, made him think of a large maze.

Wandering first in one direction, then another, he finally found what he was looking for. The pet shop. He reasoned it might be good for a quarter of an hour or so. "Want to see puppies, Robin?"

"Seepuppies," she exclaimed, running the two words into one. "Seepuppies!"

"Okay, we'll see puppies." There was an eager Lhasa apso leaping up and down in the window as they entered. "I just hope the puppies don't regret it."

He took her deep into the store, where the dogs were housed in cages behind sliding glass doors. Robin squealed with excitement as soon as she saw them. Lunging forward in his arms, she patted the glass just the way she had his face last night.

Her excitement was infectious. "I think I'm jealous, Robin."

The dark-haired attendant in the corner stopped sweeping and retired her broom. "Would your little girl like to pet one of the dogs?"

"Pet, pet, pet," Robin echoed, bouncing up and down in his arms.

He was about to say she wasn't his little girl, but that would be getting into an unnecessary conversation. "No, that's too much trouble."

But the attendant was already unlocking the sliding doors. "No trouble at all. It's a slow morning."

Before he knew it, Malcolm was holding not only Robin but a cocker spaniel puppy, as well. It was hard to say which one wiggled more.

The attendant laughed and led him to what she told him was a petting booth in the back. He thought of some of the men he'd shared his career with who would have had another use for a booth with that name, and bit back a grin.

The cocker spaniel looked to be the same age in dog years as Robin was in human. As the puppy licked her, her childish laughter tightened around Malcolm's heart. He held the feeling to him, disregarding the accompanying pain. He knew that would lay sole claim to him later, but for now, he allowed himself to enjoy Robin.

In his naivete, it seemed harmless enough.

Chapter Seven

Malcolm's experience with the shooting water fountain didn't go quite as well.

After managing to successfully separate Robin from the cocker spaniel before she squeezed the puppy in half, Malcolm took her outside. They wandered past the fountain just as it sent several streams of water shooting up in the air.

The architect, Malcolm assumed, had meant the sight to be an interesting one. For a two-year-old given to a deep-rooted obsession with all things liquid, it was nothing short of fascinating.

Several very plaintive squeals and frantic tugging on his shirt told Malcolm that Robin was eager to play in the water. He saw no harm in letting her dip her hands into it.

He'd forgotten that Murphy's Law always lurked in the shadows, especially when it came to children.

With his arm securely wrapped around her waist, Malcolm sat down on the rim of the fountain and allowed Robin to splash to her heart's content. In his innocence, he thought he had all bases covered, but it had been a while since he had been pitted against a two-year-old, and he discovered that he was sorely unprepared.

As Robin tried to wiggle forward to grab a trickle of water coming from the closest jet, the trickle turned into a gusher. Suddenly, water was shooting up at least ten feet overhead. The trajectory was aimed for the center of the fountain—unless interfered with.

And Robin interfered with it.

Malcolm pulled her away, but it was too late. She was soaked to the skin. Surprised, she sputtered.

Malcolm expected wails and tears next. Instead, Robin blinked her eyes, her dark lashes sending the water flying, and giggled. With renewed zest, she clapped her hands, applauding the water.

"Mo'," she ordered Malcolm, kicking her feet and trying to get loose. "Mo'."

"No 'mo','" he informed her, but the smile that curved the corners of his mouth took the edge off his reprimand. He shook his head as he rose with her. "Your mother didn't tell me you were part guppy."

"Puppy." Her head spun around in the direction of the pet store. "Seepuppy."

"No, not 'puppy.' 'Guppy.'" It was useless to argue with her. In that, he mused, she was a lot like her mother. "Never mind."

Holding her against him, Malcolm picked up the diaper bag with a resigned sigh. He would soon be as wet as she was. He might as well head back to the car and change her there. He didn't relish what that was going to do to the upholstery.

"If you're looking for somewhere to change her, the ground-floor men's room in that department store has a changing table."

The suggestion came from behind him. Malcolm turned to see a harried-looking man standing there with a child attached to each hand. They were tugging him in opposite directions. He was holding fast, but it didn't look as if he could hold on for long.

With a commiserating smile, the man nodded toward the store Malcolm had passed earlier in his search for the pet shop.

A changing table in the men's room. Well, there was something he wouldn't have expected. Times had certainly changed since Sally was born. Malcolm was too caught up in the immediate situation to realize that for once, the memory of his daughter didn't dredge up a quick shot of pain with it.

"Thanks." Slinging the bag over his shoulder, Malcolm left the man in his wake and headed toward the men's room of the department store.

Once organized, he changed Robin from top to bottom in under five minutes. It was like riding a bike, he mused, putting a fresh pair of socks on the wiggling feet. Some things you just never forgot.

His friends had all kidded him about becoming Sally's nursemaid, but he had let the ribbing go without comment. Let them talk, he'd thought. He didn't care. He had loved it, every part of being a parent. Even the diaper changing. And especially the part of holding a dry, sweet-smelling baby in his arms.

Like now.

"There." He scooped Robin up with one hand and picked up the bag with the other. "I think you're presentable enough for your mother." Pushing the swinging door open with his back, Malcolm glanced down at his own damp shirt. He ignored the curious look a salesman gave him as he walked out. "Hopefully, she won't notice that you've got on a different outfit and I'm dripping."

She did, but not at first.

The altitude of the cloud Christa was occupying would make it difficult for her to notice mundane things like a damp shirt, even if it was on a torso as muscular as his. Euphoria temporarily blocked her vision. Christa left the office building humming and fairly skipped down the stone steps.

The interview had gone so well, they had offered her the job on the spot.

She was pleased to see that Malcolm and Robin were waiting for her in the parking lot, standing beside his car. She didn't want to waste a minute before sharing this with them.

"Congratulate me," she called out as she hurried over. God, she felt so good, she could hug the whole world. In lieu of that, Robin and Malcolm would do just fine.

Robin squealed gleefully. Malcolm's reaction was a little more reserved and yet all the more intense for that. She took a step back.

She'd overwhelmed him. Again.

"Why?" He'd thought that she always looked happy. He'd been wrong. She was downright radiant right now.

"As of 10:49, I am an employed woman." She tossed her hair over her shoulder, her eyes dancing. "They're revamping their accounting department, and I start in three weeks."

And then she looked at them, really looked. Robin had been wearing a pink dress when she'd left. Now she had on green rompers. And Malcolm had a dark stain on his otherwise light blue shirt.

As she took Robin into her arms, she touched the front of Malcolm's shirt. She hadn't imagined it. It was wet. "What happened to you two?"

His mouth curved ruefully. "It was such a nice day, we decided to take a swim," he quipped, then shrugged. "She reached into the fountain and got caught in one of the sprays as it went off. But she's okay." He laughed to himself. "She didn't cry. She wanted 'mo'.'"

The fountain. That would explain why his shirt was damp. Except for the ends of Robin's hair, she was completely dry.

"You changed her."

The awe in her voice made him uncomfortable. What did she expect him to do with Robin when she was wet, pop her in a microwave?

"Obviously. Wasn't that what the spare clothing in the bag was for?"

"Well, yes." She always had the clothes along in case she had to change Robin. She hadn't even thought of anyone else utilizing them. In all their time together, Jim had never so much as put Robin's shoes on her, much less changed her. "But I didn't think that you'd—" Christa broke off, seeing that she was embarrassing him. "You must be the handiest man I know."

Or the most easily manipulated, Malcolm added silently. "Seemed like the thing to do at the time," he muttered.

Robin began to wiggle in her arms. "Seepuppies, seepuppies!" She pointed all around.

It took Christa a moment to make out the words. "Puppies?" The blond head bobbed up and down.

Christa looked to Malcolm for an explanation. "What's she talking about?"

He hoped she wasn't going to make a big deal out of this, too. "I took her to the pet store. I think Robin and a cocker spaniel fell mutually in love." Christa was looking at him in that way of hers, that way that said another round of gratitude was about to come spilling out of her mouth. Thinking quickly, he changed the topic. "So, you got the job?"

His question brought back the wondrous elation she felt. It buoyed her, but not quite as much, she realized, as the feeling she'd experienced last night when he had kissed her. "Yes."

That was fast, he thought. "They must have been pretty impressed with you."

Her references and credentials were of a high caliber, but she knew that wasn't necessarily always enough. "Just a matter of being in the right place at the right time." Her eyes examined his face. She thought of yesterday, of the way he had rescued Robin, and became humble all over again. She would never stop being grateful to him for that. "Like you."

He had been in the right place at the right time before, and had been unable to do anything. He shrugged away her comment. "That all depends on your point of view."

She didn't know if he was being modest or evasive, but it was obvious that he didn't want to discuss it. Christa felt too happy to mar today for either of them. "Would you like to come with us and celebrate?"

Yes, he thought, he would, which was why he turned her down.

"Sorry," he answered crisply, unlocking the car doors, "but I do have a business to run."

She flushed. So far, she'd done nothing but impose on him. Christa opened the passenger side and pushed forward the front seat. Lifting Robin up, she placed the little girl into the car seat that was wedged into the minuscule space behind the front seats.

"I'm sorry," she apologized as she sat down herself. Christa buckled up just as Malcolm turned the key in the ignition. "That was thoughtless of me. It's just that I'm so excited." Her contrition melted in the face of her happiness. "Everything's opening up for me. Now I can buy a Big Wheel."

He guided the car out of the lot, waiting for a car to pass before driving onto the street. "Excuse me?"

"A Big Wheel," she repeated. "One of those kid tricycles." She lowered her voice. "I wanted to get it for Robin's birthday."

He laughed. Another woman would have been talking about getting herself clothes or some longed-for appliance, if not a piece of jewelry. Not a tricycle. "Think big, don't you?"

She didn't take it as a criticism. "In a way. The best things in life are the little things." She glanced over her shoulder at Robin. The little girl's eyes were drifting shut. Obviously, her morning with Malcolm had tired her out. "They make the big picture better, don't you think?"

He thought of his own daughter. Of the way he'd been content just to watch her sleep. Life on the road had made things like that even more precious. "Yeah, I do."

He said nothing more, and for several minutes, the silence encompassed them. She didn't feel uncomfortable in it, she realized. It wasn't a pregnant silence or an awkward one; it was just a natural lull in the conversation.

The thought made her smile.

He was aware of her smiling at him, could *feel* her smiling. "What?"

Christa thought it prudent not to explain what she was thinking. He might think she was crazy. "I can pay you now."

He knew how important it was to feel as if you could pay your own way. It had always meant a great deal to him, even in the early years. "Meaning you weren't going to before?"

She couldn't tell if he was joking or not, but didn't take any chances. She didn't want him getting the wrong impression.

"No, I meant that until now it was going to be broken up in probably a hundred installments." She slanted a look at his face. It was impassive. No surprise there. "I think you knew that. Now I might even be able to pay you off before the end of the month."

He bit the inside of his cheek. "You haven't seen my bill yet."

She shifted, her eyes wide, serious. She didn't think he was capable of putting her on. "That big?"

He laughed. "Anyone ever tell you that you're gullible?"

His words stirred an unpleasant memory. Her voice grew quiet as she answered. "Yes, my ex-husband. Except that I turned out to be the one who had a firmer hold on reality than he did."

He turned his eyes back on the road as he eased his foot off the brake. "Sorry, didn't mean to bring up anything painful."

She shrugged. "That's all right, you didn't know. Besides, that's all in the past now. 'That which doesn't kill us makes us stronger,' right?"

"Maybe," he muttered.

Before she could comment, Malcolm turned up the radio, doing away with the necessity of carrying on a conversation.

When they reached Christa's condo, Malcolm stopped the car and got out.

"You don't have to bother getting out and helping me," she protested.

"I can't very well just eject you out of your seats while I'm driving," he answered. "The mechanism's jammed."

Christa laughed as she deposited her bag on the sidewalk. "I like that."

He stared at her. "Like what?"

"The way your eyes soften when you're kidding. It doesn't make you look quite as dangerous."

"I thought women were supposed to like dangerous men," he said as he pushed the passenger seat down and took Robin out, car seat and all. He set both on the ground.

"That's only in books. In real life, a woman likes a nice, dependable man—who kisses dangerous," she added with a mischievous grin. *The way he did.*

"Who kisses dangerous?" he echoed. That was a new one on him.

She nodded and then, before she could think better of it and retreat, her arms went around his neck and she showed him. "Like this."

Like a brushfire igniting summer-baked grass, the kiss combusted and took off, sucking them both in greedily.

She felt so good against him. Good and soft and wondrous. His hands snaked around her waist, pressing her to him, then roamed her back, as if memorizing every inch, every curve, every nuance.

Hunger, deep and gut wrenching, seized him, asking to be fed. Demanding it.

He struggled to keep it from consuming him, to keep from giving in to it, even a little.

He succeeded.

And failed.

Because it took a piece of his soul with it as he fought. Took it from him and gave it to her. He could feel the force of the explosion in his veins.

Finally, with his willpower about to crack in half, Malcolm placed his hands on her waist again and drew her away from him.

The impish smile on her lips was blurred with the imprint of his mouth. It made him hungry again. And stoked the embers of his guilt.

He was alive and feeling things. And his wife and daughter weren't.

Malcolm found his voice, and it rumbled up from the depths of him. "So that's a dangerous kiss?"

She felt shaky and reveled in it. This new sensation was one she could very easily become addicted to. "Yes," she whispered. "Very."

He cleared his throat. "Then we'd better not do it again."

It wasn't what she wanted to hear. "There is a certain attraction to danger."

"Yes, I know. That's why we better not do it again."

Christa could feel the sting of tears in her eyes and didn't really know why they were there or why she was suddenly devastated on this day that had gone so well for her.

Blinking them away, she turned to take Robin out of her seat. Behind her, she could hear Malcolm getting into his car.

She turned around quickly before he could leave.

"I'll be back to work on the van tonight" was all Malcolm said before he pulled away.

"I'm counting on it," she murmured to herself, watching him drive away.

It was past eight o'clock, and Malcolm still hadn't showed up.

He wasn't going to come, she thought, dejection wafting through her. It was all her own fault. She'd probably scared him off.

She'd been so certain, as she'd left Las Vegas and Jim, that all she wanted out of life was Robin and a decent job so that she could take care of them both. Now she wasn't so sure. Now her narrow wish list had grown to include one more thing.

One more person.

Restless, she began straightening the living room. Robin's toys had managed to find their way everywhere. How could one little girl make so much mess?

She needed a system, Christa mused, pushing the toys into a corner. A system that—

She cocked her head, listening. Those weren't crickets, she realized. Not unless the crickets were using power tools.

Pushing the plastic blocks to the corner with her toe, Christa went to the window. There, beneath the combined pool of moonlight, street lamp and the work light he had brought with him, was Malcolm.

Stripped down to the waist in deference to the hot night, he was working on her van. A sparkle of joy exploded within her. He'd come after all.

How long had he been out there?

Christa opened the door and went outside. The unex-
pected humidity of the day had passed, leaving only the
dry heat of night in its wake.

Not so dry, she mused, seeing the sheen of sweat on his
body. She felt guilty that he was working when he should
be home unwinding. She felt guiltier that she was glad he
wasn't there but here.

He knew she was coming before she ever approached.
Even if he hadn't heard the front door open and close, he
would have known. His peripheral vision was excellent.
His sense of smell was even better, and she was wearing
that cologne again, the one that reminded him of the
flowers they handed out in the winner's circle.

Christa hooked her fingers in the loops of her denim
shorts. "I didn't hear you drive up."

He didn't bother looking up. It was safer that way.
"Roaring engines are for kids."

Maybe, but that still didn't explain things. "Why
didn't you knock?"

He reached for another wrench, a smaller one, as he
lifted a shoulder. "Didn't see the point. Told you I'd be
back to work on the van." He raised his head for only a
moment. Just as he thought, she was underdressed again.
"And I am."

"Can I get you anything?" She was addressing the top
of his head. Was it her imagination, or was he purposely
avoiding her eyes?

He waved her back. "You can get out of my light."

"Sorry." She shifted, taking a step back. But she didn't
leave as he had hoped.

Instead, she just persisted. "Something to drink?
Eat?" He wasn't paying any attention. That much wasn't
her imagination. "Sing to you?"

He looked up, brows drawn together in confusion. "What?"

She grinned. At least she'd gotten him to look at her. "I was waiting for you to answer. I thought maybe you weren't listening."

He grunted something unintelligible and went back to work.

Giving up trying to play the hostess, Christa sat down on the curb. Bracing her hands behind her on the sidewalk, she stretched out her long, tanned legs in front of her. The stars were out, and it was a gorgeous night.

He told himself he didn't notice, but that damn peripheral vision of his was getting in the way again. He noticed, all right. Noticed too much for their own good.

She glanced over her shoulder at him. She wondered if he would continue to work in silence if she didn't say anything. He had something attached to a portable generator and it was humming, but even the noise couldn't seem to cut into the silence between them.

"I thought you weren't coming."

"I said I was, didn't I?" Damn, it was just as he'd thought. The radiator had a small crack in it. She was going to need a new one. The number of things wrong with the van was mounting steadily. "I always finish what I start."

Christa had already figured that out on her own. "Admirable quality."

Why did he feel so irritated when she complimented him? It wasn't rational—neither was the way he reacted to her.

"Just makes good sense if you're a businessman." Because the silence bothered him, he decided to explain why he'd been so late. "The engine I was overhauling took longer than I thought it might."

She merely nodded. It didn't matter why he was late, just that he was here.

She lifted her hair from the back of her neck, then let it drop again. As she leaned back, her halter top strained against her breasts, tempting him. Seducing him.

He dropped the wrench he was holding, then muttered a curse under his breath as he bent to pick it up.

"Do you have to sit there like that?" he asked curtly.

"No, I can stand." She was already rising to her feet.

He spoke before he weighed his words. "I was thinking more in terms of your going away."

It was just his defense mechanism talking. She wasn't going to allow the words to hurt. "I thought you might like company while you work."

He struggled to ignore her, to ignore the sensual images that were beginning to appear in his mind. "Well, I don't."

She cocked her head, trying to understand. "Why are you so snappish tonight?"

He stuck to his story. "Because you're getting in my way."

She wasn't in his light and she certainly wasn't in the path of his toolbox. She splayed her hands out innocently. "I'm standing right here."

He raised his eyes to her face. She'd played on his mind all day. All last night. Giving him no peace. "You're still getting in my way."

Christa shook her head, lost. "I think we're having an argument here and I'm not sure what it's about. Could you give me some ground rules?"

He sighed impatiently, tossing the wrench into the box before picking up another one. The look he directed at her before going to back to work was dark and edgy.

"I don't know what you're talking about. I just asked you to go inside, that's all."

"You asked me to go away. There's a difference."

He blew out a breath. He wasn't going to get sucked into this discussion. "If you say so."

She didn't want to argue. She wanted to be friends. Why wouldn't he let her? At a loss how to smooth things over, she fell back on the one thing they agreed on.

"You made a great impression on Robin today. She kept asking about 'Man.'"

The comment brought the first grin from him that she had seen this evening. "She's a terrific little girl."

"Yes, she is." Given a toehold, Christa quickly built on it. "But a lot of men are uncomfortable around children. You have a real knack." She ventured further again. "Do you have any children of your own?"

His face clouded as he continued working. "No."

"But you did," she guessed. She knew she was pushing, but she couldn't help herself. She had to know. For his sake.

It wasn't fair to Sally to deny her existence. "Yes, I did."

She knew it. "A daughter?"

"Yeah."

The word fairly assaulted her, warning her to back off. Christa pressed on. "What happened to her?"

He raised his head and glared at her. "Answers about my private life aren't included in the work, Christa."

It was the first time he'd said her name. She wished it hadn't been in anger. "I am aware of that. And I'm not being nosy. I think you need to talk about her."

Cereal-box psychology. "Well, I don't, so I guess this is a Mexican standoff." Malcolm wiped his hands on the back of his jeans, then slammed the hood shut. "Look, it's really getting late, and I don't want to do a shoddy job. Maybe we'd better postpone this until the weekend when I can do this in daylight."

He wasn't leaving because of the lack of light; he was leaving because she was getting too close to something, something he wanted to leave alone.

"All right."

Disconnecting the generator, Malcolm placed it in his car. "So I'll see you Saturday." Not waiting for an answer, he tossed the toolbox into his car and got in.

She came around to his side quickly. "I really wasn't prying."

He gunned his engine in reply, drowning her out. "You could have fooled me."

He drove away before she could protest his assessment. There'd been pain in his eyes when she'd asked about his daughter. Pain he had to bring into the light and deal with before he could begin to heal.

With a sigh, she turned around and went back into her house. For now, she was at a loss as to how to help him. But there was always tomorrow. Something would come to her tomorrow. It had to.

Chapter Eight

Whistling tunelessly between his teeth, Jock Peritoni pulled his two month old, gleaming dark blue four-wheel-drive up behind the garage and got out. He spent a moment admiring his pride and joy before he flipped the lever that locked both doors.

Still whistling, he turned to circumvent the wide, squat building where he worked when he noticed that Malcolm's LeMans was parked at the far end. The black car was almost obscured by the low-dipping branches of the California pepper trees that lined the back fence.

He'd come in early, expecting to find no one but Sam, the night attendant on the job. Was something wrong? Curious, Jock scratched his head as he walked into the work pit. He found Malcolm bending over a beige BMW.

"Boss?"

Malcolm was just finishing up a work order he'd started a little after six this morning. The mug of coffee standing on the side worktable had long since grown cold waiting for him to remember it. He spared Jock a look in response to the greeting but said nothing.

It didn't faze Jock. He was accustomed to doing the talking for both of them. Sauntering over, he peered around Malcolm's shoulder to see what he was doing. Malcolm had hands like a magician when it came to cars. None better. Jock had picked up a great deal in the past few months.

A lopsided grin spread over the thin lips. "I thought maybe you'd be coming in late again today, like yesterday." He held up a hand, quickly realizing his mistake as Malcolm's brow rose. "Not that there's anything wrong about you coming in late. I think it's great." And he did. You couldn't very well slack off once in a while if the boss was always there, working. "A boss should kick back once in a while, and you've been working awfully hard. Dad said you always worked hard."

"Dad" was Wally Peritoni, one of the reigning aces of the racing circuit, a living icon to all the would-be racers who came after him. Wally had taken Malcolm under his wing when he was new to the racing world. There had been no reason for Wally to have put himself out that way, but he had. He had taken a hopelessly wet-behind-the-ears kid and turned him into a pro.

Wally had become the father Malcolm had never had. Malcolm would always be grateful to him.

The way, he thought suddenly, Christa would always be to him.

"Your dad never expected anything else," Malcolm said matter-of-factly. He pushed the oil tray under the car with the tip of his boot. "Speaking of hard work, the work orders are piling up. Take your pick. We've got a full schedule today."

Jock took a look at the various eight-by-ten sheets hanging haphazardly on the bulletin board as he walked past it. He headed to the tiny rest room in the rear, holding his dark blue work shirt in his hand.

"You know, there's enough work here for another guy, too. My cousin Billy..."

Malcolm nodded. He knew that Jock was capable of launching into a ten-minute monologue on his cousin's virtues if he let him. Jock could talk nonstop about almost anything. Even so, Malcolm had taken a liking to the tall, scrawny nineteen-year-old.

Just as Wally had taken a liking to him all those years ago. Funny thing about life. It seemed to go in circles. And he felt himself on the verge of one.

"Okay, send him around."

"Will do." Jock beamed. As he entered the rest room, he raised his voice. "Dad says to tell you hi."

"Hi," Malcolm muttered under his breath.

He shook his head as he removed a clogged, filthy oil filter. According to the sticker on the inside of the driver's door, the filter should have been changed ten thousand miles ago. Didn't people realize how much trouble they could avoid if they just changed their car's oil regularly?

Obviously not. Look at Christa.... He shut down the thought. Damn it all. Ever since last night, she'd been popping up in his mind like a piece of toast in a malfunctioning toaster.

He swore and threw the filter into a large barrel that served as a receptacle for discarded parts. It clanged, reaching bottom.

Jock poked his head out of the rest room, curious, as the loud noise echoed through the enclosure. Malcolm's expression was unchanged. Jock wondered if something had set him off.

Walking out, Jock slid his long, thin hands into the waistband of his jeans, tucking his shirt in. "Dad wanted me to ask you if you think you're *ever* going to come back to racing. He says that it's been a long—"

"Tell him no," he said tersely, wondering why everyone was so concerned with what he was doing with himself. "I don't ever plan to go back."

Malcolm paused, annoyed. He hadn't meant to snap like that. What had happened three years ago wasn't Jock's fault. And what had happened yesterday sure wasn't Jock's fault, either.

The blame was all his in both cases. In the latter case, he was opening up a door that led to a place he had no business entering. He couldn't allow himself to begin all that again. It wasn't right.

A vague shrug rolled along his shoulders by way of an apology. "Sorry, I'm a little edgy this morning."

Jock looked stunned. Malcolm never apologized; he just let incidents fade away. "Sure thing, I understand. Been edgy myself now and again. Why, last night, I did the damnedest thing right after I left here. I got into my car and—"

There was no telling how long Jock would have gone on talking if the sight of the woman hadn't stopped him.

Her eyes were on Malcolm, and she was coming straight at them. Jock cleared his throat. "Um, boss?"

Malcolm had already tuned Jock out. He always did when the boy launched into a long story. Jock had to call his name twice before he responded.

"Now what?" Malcolm lifted the pan of discarded oil and went around to the rear of the work area. He poured the contents into the lined container the city provided.

"I think someone's here to see you."

Emerging, Malcolm looked at him. Jock nodded toward the woman who had entered the restricted work area. She was pushing a stroller before her.

Christa.

Exasperated, Malcolm put down the pan and dried his hands on a rag. The look he greeted her with was far from friendly. "Don't you know better than to walk in here?"

Well, he wasn't a hypocrite; that was for sure. He talked to her in public just the same way he did in private. "Are you going to bite my head off today, too?"

Maybe his warning had been a little harsh, he acknowledged. "This area is restricted," he explained. "That means only employees are allowed inside."

Christa made a show of looking around. There were five lifts side by side, and although there was a car on each one, they were standing idle. No one else was in the work area save for them and the tall, gangly youth who looked as if he was absorbing every word they said.

"Nothing's going on," she countered.

Malcolm tossed the rag on the scarred worktable. "It's the rule. It should be obeyed."

"But you bend rules, or you used to."

He quirked a brow, silently asking her to explain.

Walked right into that one, didn't I? Christa thought ruefully. Well, she might as well tell him and hope he wouldn't take it the wrong way.

"My father found an old article on you in a copy of *Sports Weekly.* I told him that you'd rescued his granddaughter." Her voice picked up speed as her explanation became more complicated. "He was going through a stack of his old magazines while he was in bed when he spotted the article. He's better, by the way," she added as a postscript, making Malcolm's head spin a little.

She pressed her lips together, debating saying anything further, then forged ahead. "I read the article. There was a photo of you and your wife and daughter." Her voice had grown soft, understanding. "You made a nice family."

He recalled the article. It had come out a month before the accident.

"Yeah, we did." He cut her off before she could ask any more questions. "What are you doing here? Your father drop you off?" He looked out into the large lot, trying to locate the Jaguar.

She shook her head. "No, I walked." It was, after all, a little more than a mile, and the exercise helped her think.

Suddenly nervous, she ran her hand along the top of the stroller. The walk had lulled Robin to sleep. The little girl sat in her stroller, her head lolled to one side, a tiny trickle of drool sliding out of one corner of her mouth.

"I came to apologize about yesterday," she began. "If I did something wrong—"

"If?" he echoed incredulously. Taking Christa by the arm, he drew her aside so that Jock couldn't hear. He glanced down at Robin, but she was still asleep. "*If* you did something wrong?"

Christa had a feeling that the apology wasn't going to go quite the way she'd planned, but she stood her ground.

"Yes, *if*," she repeated firmly. "It all depends on your point of view. From mine, I was just trying to a help a friend—"

They'd gone over all that before. "I told you, I don't need any more friends. And what I especially don't need is to get involved with a woman who won't stop asking questions—''

Her eyes widened as she heard only one phrase. ''Are we?''

The abrupt intrusion made him lose his train of thought. ''Are we what?''

''Involved?''

Her voice was quiet, moving along his skin like velvet. The early-morning breeze played with the ends of her hair. They floated about her face like blond streamers, beckoning to him.

''No,'' he snapped automatically. Blowing out a breath, he stared into her eyes. They both knew his answer wasn't true. ''Yes,'' he relented. ''I suppose that we are.'' And that was just the trouble. ''In a superficial sort of way,'' he qualified.

''Well, it's not going to get any less shallow if we can't talk to each other.''

He snorted and turned away from her. If he didn't get back to his work, he was going to fall behind. ''You don't seem to have any trouble talking.''

Tyler had once told her she could talk the ears off a brass monkey, but that wasn't the point. Talking and being heard were two very different things.

''But I seem to have trouble getting answers.'' Ignoring his edict, she followed him to the rear of the work area, pushing the stroller. ''I know this is probably no comparison, but I've been on the other side of pain, I know what you're going through.''

When he swung around, the look in his fathomless eyes was so black, it made her take a step back. ''No, you don't. You haven't a clue.'' He didn't shout; he didn't even raise his voice. He didn't have to. The look on his face made his point for him. ''Until you've been a permanent resident in hell, you really don't have a clue at all."

She inclined her head as his words registered. Maybe she'd made a mistake coming here. A mistake thinking she could get through to him and find a way to help him. Maybe there *was* no getting through to him.

Pivoting the stroller on its rear wheels, she turned it around.

"I'm sorry I bothered you," she told him quietly. "And I'm sorry about last night."

Yes, so was he. Sorry it had happened. Sorry that he wasn't free to enjoy it the way he should. Sorry he couldn't be like other men. "Which part?"

She wasn't going to say specifically, because she didn't regret the kiss. And she didn't regret trying to get close to another human being. The only thing she did regret was that she couldn't—that he wouldn't allow it.

Christa opted for vagueness. "Any part that hurt you." With that, she began to walk quickly away.

The set of her shoulders nudged at his guilt. He didn't want to hurt her. None of this was her fault.

Even as he called to her, he knew he was going to be sorry he did. But he didn't seem to be able to just let it go. "Christa."

She turned, waiting.

"I'll be there tonight to work on the van."

He made her feel like a damn tennis ball, being lobbed back and forth over the net. Right now, the ball was back on her side.

How did she keep it there?

Christa smiled in response, then kept on walking. "I'll look forward to it."

"That'll make one of us," he muttered under his breath. But he was lying.

"She's nice," Jock declared, bounding over as soon as Christa was out of earshot.

He was in no mood to listen to Jock extol Christa's virtues. The kid could come through with a list even if he didn't know her.

"Go call the tire company and see what's keeping that order. It should have arrived here last night," Malcolm instructed. "And call your cousin. Ask him if he can come down for an interview this afternoon."

"Yes, *sir*." Jock grinned broadly as he went to do what he was told.

With any luck, Malcolm thought impatiently, he could pry her out of his mind long enough to get some work done.

He didn't feel very lucky.

Jonas McGuire let the filmy curtain fall back into place as he muttered something to himself. Hands wrapped around the mug of coffee his daughter had poured for him, he meandered back to the kitchen. It was Saturday, and Christa was working on lunch.

He eyed his only daughter with the feelings of a man who was vaguely aware that he hadn't done as good a job as he would have liked in raising her. He'd always been so busy just being a cop. It had been Martha's job to raise the kids. And then Martha had died and left it all up to him. It sure as hell hadn't been easy, even though Christa had been a good kid.

Jonas jerked a thumb toward the front. "He's been out there working on that thing for over two weeks now—"

Christa dusted off her hands as she reached into the refrigerator for a carton of milk. She measured out a quarter cup and poured it into the pot on the stove. "It's only been one week," she corrected mildly.

Jonas took a sip of the inky black coffee before answering. He scowled at the correction. He hated nitpicking. "Same thing."

Christa grinned at the way he rolled over the inaccuracy. Some things, it seemed, never changed. "And you were out there for what, twenty years, giving tickets, huh?"

"Twenty-two, and don't get uppity with me, missy." He tried to maintain the frown, but watching his granddaughter out of the corner of his eye threatened to destroy his facade. Sunshine and spirit in rompers. He absolutely doted on her.

Christa held her hands up in surrender. "Wouldn't dream of it."

Jonas sat down, stretching his legs out before him. He eyed the front window, though he couldn't see out from where he sat. That Evans fella wouldn't make a bad son-in-law from what he'd read about him. "The Gentleman Racer," the article had called him. Not a bad thing, being a gentleman in this day and age.

Cocking his head just as his daughter and his granddaughter did, he watched Christa as she moved about the small kitchen.

"So what's he working on, besides the van?" It was about time Christa thought about moving on with her life, he decided. She'd wasted enough time on that no-account she'd married. Time to find a real man who wasn't afraid of working with his hands.

Christa poured out the contents of a box of spaghetti onto a plate and waited for the water-and-milk mixture to boil. "He has his own garage."

That wasn't what he was asking, and she knew it. "I read the article on him. I know what he did for a living and what he does now." Most of his information had come from Tyler, not Christa. For a chatty thing, there were times when his daughter could be annoyingly close-mouthed. "But that's not what I'm talking about." Getting up, he crossed to the stove. "Does he have any designs on you?"

She laughed softly at the question. Cutting open the small pouch with herbs and spices, she shook it into the pot. "I don't think he wants to get involved again."

Jonas was silent for a moment. He hadn't been the greatest father, but he had done his best. He'd be the first to admit that he was better at raising boys than girls. But he'd picked up some things along the way. One of which was being able to read her.

"But you do."

Christa shrugged. "Yes, eventually."

She was being deliberately vague. Jonas pinned her down. "With him."

"Maybe." She measured out a teaspoon of salt, then replaced the lid. "But it's not about what I want, it's about what he wants."

Jonas snorted. He didn't think for one minute that she believed that. If she did, she was a rarer woman than he thought she was. And a more naive one.

"Oh, no, it's always about what you women want. Men don't know what they want," he told her adamantly. "You gotta show them."

Christa laid down the spoon and laughed. Her relationship with her father had gotten better now that she was on an adult footing with him. They'd spent her teen years arguing almost nonstop. She'd grown to like him now, as well as love him.

Draping an arm around his shoulders, she leaned her head against his. "Are you letting me in on an age-old male secret?"

He shrugged off her arm and her patronizing manner. He was being serious. "Same one your mother let me in on. Up until then, I thought I knew my own mind. She showed me otherwise." His mouth curved fondly when he thought of his late wife. The years they'd spent together grew better every time he reviewed them in his mind. "It's up to you to show him."

As if she could. Christa lifted the lid and poured in the spaghetti. "You're being disloyal to your species, Dad."

He had no patience with dancing around subjects. "Hell, I'm being loyal to my own flesh and blood. You want him, go get him."

He made it sound so easy. And it wasn't. "He's not a fish, Dad."

Jonas had made up his mind about the mechanic who kept turning up in his daughter's driveway. A man didn't go out of his way like that unless he wanted something, consciously or otherwise. If it was unconscious, then someone had to be there to show him.

"Looks to me like he is. A fish out of water. I've seen the way he looks at you, at Robin. That man needs a family. You've got one. Seems to me the solution's a simple one."

With a laugh, Christa brushed his check with a kiss. "That's what I like about you, Dad. You're so uncomplicated."

He smiled and his face softened into a network of lines that had been earned through years spent out in the open.

"I'm also right." It was time some good things happened to her. She was too damn stubborn to let him do anything for her, but he could always try. "Want me to nudge him for you?"

Christa rolled her eyes. That was all she needed, a retired policeman leaning on Malcolm, asking him what his intentions were and broadly hinting that he become serious with his daughter. Malcolm would turn tail so fast they wouldn't be able to see him for the dust.

"I'm a big girl now, Dad," she assured him, patting his hand. "I can handle my own life." She saw the look in his eyes. She knew what he was thinking. "At least as well as anyone can handle theirs."

He gave her what he thought passed for an innocent look. "I didn't say anything."

"That would be a first," she murmured. Her father stuck his tongue out at her. Christa mimicked the gesture, and they both laughed.

Satisfied that the spaghetti and sauce were well on their way to becoming lunch, Christa opened the refrigerator and took out a pitcher of iced coffee. She poured some into a tall, frosted glass. It was time Malcolm took a short break. He'd been out there since before her father had arrived.

"I'm going to see if he wants something."

Jonas rose to look in on his granddaughter. She was entirely too quiet. In his experience, that usually meant trouble. "Tell him he can't have it unless he marries you first."

"Dad!"

He looked at her innocently. "Just looking out for your interests." He pocketed a couple of the chocolate-chip cookies Christa had laid out on a platter on the table. It always helped to have a bribe when you dealt with children, he mused as he walked out. Even with cute ones who resembled you.

Christa slipped on a pair of sandals before going outside. The sun had rendered the driveway too hot for bare feet. She felt guilty, having Malcolm work outside on a day like today.

As she approached, she saw the expression on his face. Had he found something else wrong with the car?

"That frown looks serious." She offered him the iced coffee.

Malcolm gratefully accepted the glass and ran it along his forehead. The cold was soothing. "I thought I'd be finished today."

Every time he repaired something, he found something else that needed to be replaced. So far, they'd gone through a water pump, hoses, fuel-injector seals and a radiator. Out of habit, he'd checked the brakes and found that they were going to have to be replaced, as well. She would have been better off getting a new van.

She exhaled the breath she was holding. She was afraid that he was going to tell her something was seriously wrong. "I still have almost two weeks before I start my new job. I can hold out." She bit her lower lip, then looked at him hopefully as he took a drink. "Provided I can get someone to take me shopping later."

Meaning him. He shook his head in disbelief. "You know, for a friendly woman, you don't seem to have any friends handy."

She grinned, looking at him. "I'm working on it."

He supposed it wouldn't kill him to take her shopping, and he had nothing planned for the rest of the day. Billy had turned out to be an excellent mechanic, and Malcolm had left Jock in charge at the garage for the day. Jock was coming along well. He took to the extra responsibility like a duck to water.

"What kind of shopping?" he asked guardedly.

"Nothing major. A couple of toy stores. Just birthday presents for Robin." She tried to remember if she'd extended an invitation to him yet. "You're invited to her party, by the way."

He didn't want to come, didn't want to sit there on the outskirts of a family, pretending to have a good time. "I'm busy."

She *hadn't* invited him. She would have remembered a refusal. "You don't know what day it is."

"Doesn't matter." He took out his dolly and squatted down. "I'm busy."

She became serious. "It does matter. She wouldn't be here if not for you."

Malcolm looked up at her from where he was sitting. When was she going to get it through her head that he didn't want her gratitude? "The guy might have abandoned the van once he realized she was in it."

If they were spinning theories, she had one of her own for him. One that sent chills down her spine. "And he could have just let her out by the side of the road, too. Or worse." She refused to allow herself to dwell on it. "He didn't exactly strike me as the type to be concerned about the welfare of a child."

Because he wouldn't get up, she got down to his level. "You saved her life, Malcolm. When are you going to accept that?"

How could he accept it? Accept the fact that he was able to save a stranger and not his own daughter? And how could he accept the fact that he was having feelings about another child, another woman, when his own family was dead, not by his hand but almost? By his lack of ability.

"Just luck," he muttered.

"And skill," she insisted.

It was an argument that wasn't meant to be won today. Christa tried for a lesser victory. She placed a hand on his shoulder. "I really would like you to take me shopping, Malcolm."

"We'll see." Before she could say anything else, he lay down on the dolly and snaked his way under her van. "Now, if you want this thing finished before the next century—"

"I know, I know, get out of your light."

With a dramatic sigh, she turned to walk back into the house. Behind her, she could have sworn she heard Malcolm laughing softly to himself.

It was a start.

Chapter Nine

Malcolm had never been one for malls. Even in the best of times, shopping was something that was way down on his list of things he liked to do. Right before having a root canal and after having his teeth cleaned.

There was absolutely no reason, then, why he should have agreed to this. It wasn't as if she had held a gun to his head or even used her feminine wiles—something he imagined she had in abundant supply, though he hadn't seen a blatant demonstration yet.

All she had done was simply ask, and he had heard himself saying yes. Maybe he'd been inhaling too many gasoline fumes lately.

Or maybe, kissing Christa, holding Robin in his arms, had rattled him down to his foundation and caused all the old rules to be overthrown.

Whatever the reason, he had been following her around now for more than three hours. Three hours in one crowded mall after another, and she was showing absolutely no indication of slowing down.

They walked out of Tots 'n' Togs, a store that only sold toddler apparel and whose prices were geared for people who had money they didn't know what to do with. He'd just watched Christa spend five minutes looking lovingly at a red velvet dress before bracing her shoulders and leaving the store.

"The dress was overpriced," he told her as they crossed the store's threshold. The first bars of "Mary Had a Little Lamb" accompanied them out.

"Way overpriced," she agreed.

He heard the longing. "And Robin could only wear it for a couple of months at best."

"At best," she echoed.

Christa looked over her shoulder into the store. The dress they were talking about was hanging out on display, the centerpiece of a miniature scene depicting Christmas morning. That alone had turned Malcolm off. It was July, for Pete's sake; why rush things?

"But you still want it." It wasn't a guess—he saw it in her eyes.

It didn't make any sense, and yet, in a strange way, he could understand her feelings. That would have worried him if he had thought about it.

She offered him a rueful smile. She knew wanting the dress was silly and extravagant. Still, she wished she had the money to indulge herself. She could just picture Robin in it. "'Ah, but a man's reach should exceed his grasp, or what's a heaven for?'"

"I don't think Browning was talking about overpriced clothes."

She looked at him in surprise. "You know Browning?"

"Not personally." His formal education had stopped at high school because of lack of funds, but his private thirst for knowledge had continued. He'd appeased it by putting together an extensive library over the years.

The dry comment had her laughing. "Sorry, I just didn't picture you as the poetry type."

A woman pushing a side-by-side stroller bumped into him. His grasp tightened on the packages he was holding. "Just because I don't spout it doesn't mean I don't know it."

She looked at him, an amused expression on her face. He had a point. "You really are a surprise to me, Malcolm."

"Yeah, to me, too." He shook his head as he looked around. The level of noise had been steadily growing with each mall they had gone to. It seemed that the later the hour, the more shoppers came out of the woodwork. "I haven't the faintest idea what I'm doing here."

Someone else jostled him, sending to the floor one of the packages he was holding.

Christa pivoted, picking the bag up before Malcolm could reach it. "Tired?" she asked sympathetically. He did look a little out of his element.

He was way past tired, but he supposed there was no point in mentioning that. Especially when she wasn't. "Amazed."

He'd grunted at every outfit she'd shown him in the store and said that taking the catalog Tots 'n' Togs offered home with her was a waste of her time and paper in general. She saw nothing that would have captured his amazement.

"At what?" Moving quickly, she took the lead and forged a path through the crowd. He followed in her wake as she wove her way to the underground-parking structure where they had left his car.

"You."

Surprised, she paused at the mall exit. "Me? Why?"

He pushed on the door and held it open with his back. Before Christa could enter, a woman with twin boys came barreling through. *Why would anyone do this to themselves willingly?* he wondered. "Don't you ever slow down?"

She laughed lightly. He hadn't seen anything yet. "Only when I run out of energy."

The door slammed behind them as they began the hunt for his car. "Which would be—?"

Mentally, she counted off the rows as they walked. The car was five aisles over and seven cars from the end. "Not anytime soon. This feels wonderful." She slid the handles of one shopping bag farther up her wrist to keep them from digging in. "I'm having a hard time not buying everything."

He thought of the accumulated loot that was already in his trunk, bought at various shops in the three malls.

"I noticed." Seeing the car, he quickened his stride until he reached it. Juggling the load, he unlocked the door. "You planning to work your way up the coast?"

She looked behind the seats. It was getting pretty full. But she was buying gifts not only from herself, but from her father and brothers, as well. Not a shopper among them, they simply handed her the money and told her to get Robin "something nice."

Christa felt it her honor bound duty to do just that.

Placing her two shopping bags beside the one with the large white teddy bear sticking out of it, she looked at Malcolm. "Just one more store, I promise."

No was the easiest word in the world to utter, as well as one of the shortest, yet he couldn't manage to say it to her.

"All right. One more." With a sigh, Malcolm got into the car and waited until she seated herself beside him. "You really are having fun, aren't you?"

Enthusiasm highlighted her face. "Yes, I am. I can't imagine anything I'd rather do than spend my money on Robin." She thought of the first store they had gone to. They'd walked into a huge summer-clearance sale. "She's going to look adorable in those dresses I got for her."

"When she grows into them," he said as he backed out of his spot.

One of the dresses she'd bought was for a four-year-old, but it was more than half-off and just too cute to pass up. "Planning for the future is all part of it."

Spinning the wheel, he stared straight ahead. "Yeah, except sometimes the future doesn't turn out quite the way you planned."

His words stung her conscience. She turned to him as they drove out into the daylight again. He'd probably gone shopping countless times with his wife for his daughter. "I'm sorry, I'm just thinking of myself. Is all this hard on you?"

He shrugged off her concern. As usual, it was misguided. "I never went shopping for Robin, except for the occasional souvenir when I was traveling. Shopping was my wife's job." He could feel her eyes on him. Malcolm turned to look at her as they came to a stop sign. "What?"

Her heart quickened. He hadn't even realized his mistake. "You said 'Robin.' You never went shopping for Robin," she paraphrased. "You meant Sally, didn't you?"

Malcolm flushed, annoyed at the slip and guilty because he had substituted one child for another in his subconscious. He blew out a breath. Traffic was stop-and-go to the light leading out of the maze of lanes that fed into the mall.

"Yes, I meant Sally. They're the same age, or would have been if—" Malcolm caught himself before he said too much. Christa had proved to be amazingly easy to talk to, but there were some things he just wasn't going to talk about with anyone.

"So," he said abruptly, "where's this last store we're going to?"

Christa could almost feel the wind from the door as he had shut it on her. Almost, she thought. But not quite. Maybe next time, she would be able to get into that inner sanctum where he kept his deepest feelings, his deepest hurts.

Looking straight ahead, she pointed down the street. "Just past the main intersection. On your left. You can't miss it. The letters are three feet high, or they look like it. Toyland," she said, adding the name for his benefit.

"Toyland," he muttered, inching up the street. It felt as if everyone in Southern California were on the road today, bound for the same malls they were. It took five minutes to make the simple turn into the parking lot.

He wondered how far from the store he'd have to park this time.

"There," Christa announced suddenly. "Quick." She pointed to the left, and he looked to see a woman pulling out of a space that wasn't more than twelve feet from the front entrance of the store. "Before someone else gets it."

He laughed. "You would have made a great driver on the track. Good reflexes."

She smiled in response, treasuring his comment as if he had just handed her a dozen long-stemmed roses. Compliments from Malcolm were rare.

"I just didn't want you to have another long walk to the store."

"I could stay behind," he volunteered. The idea was appealing.

It was another ninety-degree day. The interior of the car would be up to a hundred and ten in minutes. "You'd roast by the time I got back."

He sighed as he got out. "That long, huh?"

She merely laughed. It told him all he needed to know. Malcolm braced himself.

It wasn't quite the ordeal he thought it would be. As soon as he walked through the automatic doors, he found himself in another world entirely. Everywhere he looked, there were toys, toys of every size and nature. The age range was from pretoddler to those who were just kids at heart.

He had feeling that Christa fell into the latter category. He never had, not even as a child. Life had been too serious, except with Gloria.

And now, with Christa.

He shook off the thought and concentrated on this newest wonderland she'd taken him to. Malcolm stood, hands on hips, surveying the store. "Wow."

The reaction was genuine and uncensored. Christa grinned, pleased.

"Haven't you ever been to one of these before?" The huge toy warehouse was part of a nationwide chain. There was a Toyland in every major city in the country. She didn't see how, as a father, he could have avoided encountering one of them, no matter where his racing had taken him to.

"No." The shelves went clear up to the ceiling. Who the hell did the inventory here? Overwhelmed, he looked at her. "Is the whole store filled with just toys?"

"Toys, clothes," she said, ticking them off on her fingers, "bikes, modeling kits—"

His eyes brightened. "Modeling kits? What kind of modeling kits?"

"Aha, we've located the inner child in the man." Christa hooked her arm through his. "All kinds of kits," she promised. "C'mon, they're on aisle 3C—unless they've switched things on me. All these stores tend to be laid out the same way," she explained. "Something comforting in familiarity, no doubt. It's not just for kids. Adults like patterns, too."

She talked so fast at times that she made his head reel. "Don't you want to see about getting Robin's toys?"

The novelty of having him actually appear interested in something was too good to pass up. "Sure, but aisle 5A isn't going anywhere. Let's go see what's on 3C." With very little coaxing, Christa drew him over to the appropriate aisle.

There was an entire wall of models. They ranged from all sorts of aircraft to cartoon characters to cars. Each had its own section.

The one devoted to cars had a wide variety to choose from. There were a number of futuristic ones and several that were rooted in the past and nostalgia. What drew his attention were the race car models.

There was one in particular. A flaming red one that resembled the very first car he'd ever driven. Malcolm took the box down from the shelf and just held it for a moment, remembering. A smile curved his mouth, though he was unaware of it.

Christa watched as he ran his hand along the side of the box. She'd never seen quite that expression on his face.

"Found something you like?" she asked softly.

Embarrassed at being caught with his emotions exposed, Malcolm shrugged. He quickly shoved the box back on the shelf, wedging it between a black Trans Am and hot pink Chevy.

"Just reminds me of the car I ran my first professional race in."

Interested, Christa picked up the box and looked at the drawing on the cover. It was realistic enough to be a photograph. "Why don't you buy it?"

Malcolm took the box from her and put it back where it belonged, on the shelf.

"Some other time." Taking her arm, he drew her away from the aisle. "Didn't you say something about getting Robin a wheelie?"

"Big Wheel," she corrected. "And yes, I did." Why was it every time she got close to him, he pulled back so abruptly it rattled her teeth? Wasn't she ever going to get past the initial hurdles?

"So when do I get to see one of these marvelous inventions?"

She couldn't believe he'd never seen one before. But she dutifully pulled him to the correct aisle. "There's one."

Like the model of the race car, it was bright red. It had oversize, cartoonlike wheels, three of them, and large blue hand grips with multicolored streamers hanging from them. The seat, yellow, was almost on the ground and, like the rest, oversize.

Malcolm could just visualize Robin on something like that, laughing, with the wind whipping around her soft blond hair.

"Oh, damn."

He turned to see Christa frowning over an empty plastic envelope. The envelope was hanging on the wall just above the tricycle. "What's the matter?"

"They're out of tickets."

He hadn't the foggiest notion what that had to do with anything. "So?"

He wasn't kidding when he said he'd never been to Toyland. "If there's no ticket," she explained patiently, "it means they're all out of Big Wheels."

Before Malcolm could tell her to buy something else, Christa was striding over to a blue-smocked salesgirl.

"Excuse me, are you out of Big Wheels?" Maybe someone had miscounted tickets, and there was one still in the back.

The girl hardly turned around. She seemed completely involved in straightening the latest action figures hanging on the end of the aisle. "You're supposed to get a ticket."

"There aren't any," Christa told her.

"Then, yeah, we're out of them."

Malcolm came up behind Christa. He didn't see what the big attraction was, but it seemed to mean something to her. "Would you mind checking the storeroom?" Quietly worded, his statement was an order, not a request.

The girl paused only to look at him before she began to move to the rear of the store. "Sure."

Five minutes later, the salesgirl returned to confirm the verdict. "We're all out." Her eyes shifted to Malcolm. "Sorry."

Christa nibbled on her lower lip. Robin was going to be disappointed. The Big Wheel was one of the few things Christa actually knew her daughter wanted. She would squeal every time a commercial for the product came on. Robin had even tried to take one away from a little girl in the park. She'd cried, "My, my," as Christa had dragged her away.

"When do you think you might get some more in?" Christa pressed.

The girl shrugged in response, then, slanting a glance at Malcolm, she called out to someone at the front desk, "Hey, Alice, are we supposed to get in Big Wheels this week?"

A disembodied voice answered over the PA, "No, they're coming in at the beginning of next month."

"Thank you," Christa murmured to the salesgirl, walking away.

Malcolm didn't understand why she looked so crushed. "You just bought her enough things for three kids and you're probably not finished. What's the problem?"

"The problem is that Robin really wants a Big Wheel. She tries to hug the TV every time she sees a commercial for one." Sighing, Christa shrugged. There were still a couple of other items she wanted to get, not to mention wrapping paper and a card. "C'mon, let's get this over with."

Malcolm fell into step beside her as she made her way over to the stuffed-animal aisle. "I thought you liked shopping."

"I do, but you look as if you need a break."

He didn't like the fact that he could be read easily. "I can keep up with you."

The smile on her lips was sassy. "Nice to know."

They weren't talking about shopping anymore, he thought. The woman should come with a code book so he could decipher her.

* * *

"At least," Malcolm amended forty-five minutes later when they were finally getting into his car again, "I *thought* I could keep up with you." She'd made short work of the aisles, selecting and discarding with the speed of a gale. Then they had spent the last twenty minutes in line. You would have thought tomorrow *was* Christmas. "I never saw anyone get such a kick out of toys before."

There was no denying that she did. There were times she felt that she got just as much pleasure playing with the toys as Robin did.

"I just want her to have everything I didn't." It was a familiar old story but no less true. "We were pretty strapped when I was young. I want Robin to have all the advantages."

It was a relief to be heading for the freeway and home. Her home, he reminded himself, not his. He still had to drop her and her countless bags off. "I never thought of having forty stuffed animals as an advantage."

Christa tossed her hair over her shoulder, feigning indignation. "I only bought four."

"Six," he corrected. "I was there, remember?"

He had been there, but he hadn't been paying attention. "Mommy Bunny and Babies was a set. They're supposed to count as one, not three."

He laughed and shook his head. "Anyone ever tell you that you have a very unique way of twisting things around to suit your purposes?"

She didn't think of it as twisting, just as seeing things differently. "It's harmless."

He thought of the way she made him feel. Twisting his thoughts around, his resolve. Making him go against his own self-imposed rules.

"Not always," he murmured under his breath.

Christa wondered if he was talking about them. She hoped so. She hoped that she was making such an impression on him that he couldn't get away from it. He was certainly having that effect on her. And she liked it.

It frightened her, the level of intensity of her reaction to him. Frightened her but excited her, as well.

In another moment, they were going to be past the mall and on the 405, heading south. "Buy you a cup of coffee, sailor?" He spent her a curious look. "C'mon, you've been such a good sport, let me buy you some coffee," she urged.

There were times she was really hard to follow. Or were those just his own tangled thoughts getting in the way? "You can pour me some at your house."

She'd pictured him opting for a quick getaway once they reached her house. After all, he'd put in over three hours squiring her around. That went way past the point of being a good sport.

Christa sat up. "You'll come over?"

"I can't very well just toss you out as I'm driving by."

No, but it could come close. She already knew that from his manner. "There's a difference between dropping me off and coming inside. Will you come over?"

"Yes, I'll come over." The traffic light blinked them onto the freeway. He thought it best to qualify his answer. "But only for a little while."

It was becoming a familiar pattern, doubting the wisdom of his own words when he was around her. He should have told her that he didn't have time to stop for coffee, that he would only be able to drop her off before leaving.

The Jaguar was there, parked at the curb. He had forgotten about her father. Christa had become an exception, but Malcolm wasn't in the mood to talk to anyone else. "Maybe I'd better take a rain check."

Now that he was here, she wasn't about to take no for an answer. He'd had his chance at the mall. "It's not supposed to rain for a long time." She'd seen the way he'd looked at the Jaguar. Christa rounded the hood to his side. "Come on in. My father isn't going to bite. We've had him defanged."

The two men had exchanged wary nods the other day, but nothing more. "I'm not afraid of your father—"

"Good, then come in." She pulled on his arm. God, but the man was stubborn. "Besides, I need help with all these packages."

"Since when?" he snorted. If he'd ever met anyone who didn't need help with anything, it was Christa. Except, perhaps, when it came to her van. . . .

"What did you do, buy out the malls?" Jonas said after he'd opened the door in response to the doorbell she'd rung with her elbow.

Malcolm stepped back, letting Christa go in first. "She tried."

"That's the trouble with women," Jonas grumbled with a shake of his head. "You give them the right to vote, the next thing you know, they're buying and selling things right out from under you."

"You can philosophize later," she told her father. "Right now, I need you to take Robin someplace while I put these away." She lifted one shopping-bag-laden wrist.

Taking Robin by the hand, Jonas muttered something under his breath about disrespectful daughters and walked off to the minuscule backyard.

"Coast clear," he sang out.

"Subtle," Christa muttered.

"I don't think she caught on," Malcolm assured her as he followed her, carrying the remainder of the bags out to the side patio.

Christa unlocked the storage unit housed beside the sliding screen door. "I can't wait for her to see all this."

Grinning, Malcolm nodded toward the backyard. "Easily granted—"

"Don't you dare," she warned. "I meant on her birthday." One by one, she piled the various bags into the storage unit.

"Maybe it's lucky you didn't get the Big Wheel," he commented as he helped her. "Where would you put it?"

Things could be rearranged to fit. If worse came to worst, she could hide some presents in her bedroom. Robin wasn't old enough to go hunting for her gifts. Yet. "I'd manage."

Yes, she would. Christa was the type to manage, Malcolm thought. He was beginning to get the feeling that no matter what, Christa would always manage. It was an admirable quality.

She had a great many admirable qualities, he mused, watching her as she stuffed package after package into the unit. Admirable qualities wrapped up in a woman with soulful eyes that seemed to get to him no matter what he did.

He wished things could be different. But wishing that meant wishing away Gloria and Sally, and he couldn't do that.

Christa turned in time to see the look in his eyes. Something was bothering him. Something she instinctively knew he wasn't going to share.

"So," she said brightly, "ready for that cup of coffee yet?"

If he was going to remain, he needed to justify it to himself. "You can bring it out to me in the driveway. Time I started on your car."

"Take a break," she suggested. "Life isn't all work, Malcolm."

"There isn't anything else."

She was losing him. Any headway she'd made was slipping out of her grasp. "Yes, there is," she insisted. "Life goes on for all of us until the day we die. Giving it up is a little like dying."

He knew what she was saying. It wasn't right to lead her on.

"This isn't any good, Christa," he told her. But even as he said it, he filled his hands with her hair and his eyes with the very sight of her. Her smile wafted to him, nudging feelings into existence that he wanted to keep buried.

They rose up despite his efforts.

"Christa, I died three years ago. I just haven't laid down yet."

"Tell me about it," she urged softly. *Please.*

He shook his head, dropping his hands to his sides. "Some other time."

She didn't want it to be some other time. "I could ask around or go to the newspaper morgue and read until my eyes are treadworn. Eventually, I could find out what it is that's eating away pieces of you. But I'd rather hear it from you."

He couldn't make himself say it. "Later," he said. "I've got work to do."

"Later," she murmured to herself as the front door closed.

He might think he was putting her off, but there *was* going to be a later, she vowed. There had to be.

Having him around, even reluctantly, made her feel safe. She knew she might be setting herself up for a fall, but there was something about Malcolm that gave her a sense of security that Jim had never created. She couldn't just let that blow away. Not without trying to hang on to it.

Chapter Ten

"So this is where you've been keeping yourself."

Wally Peritoni walked up behind Malcolm and looked around the work area. He slid his wide hands into neatly pressed tan trousers as his eyes glinted, surveying the bulletin board with its backlog of work orders. Wally had the same wiry build as his son, except that he had filled out a little with the passage of time, giving him a sturdier appearance. The wind ruffled his signature shock of white hair. It had turned prematurely white while he was in his early twenties, earning him the nickname of "Old Man." He'd liked the nickname better before it had grown closer to the truth.

Whistling tunelessly—a habit his son had picked up and perpetuated years ago—Wally gave a barely nonjudgmental shake of his head. "Waste of talent being here, Malcolm. You know that. A damn waste of talent."

Malcolm dropped the spent fuel injector into the receptacle, It had been a year since he had seen Wally. Maybe a little longer; he'd lost count. But Wally picked up the conversation as if they'd seen one another only yesterday. He had that kind of knack. "You come to harass me, Old Man?"

The pumps were thriving, and he had a healthy amount of cars waiting to be worked on, Wally noted. Still, it seemed a shame, seeing Malcolm here like this.

He moved closer and clapped a hand on Malcolm's shoulder. "No, I came to thank you for hiring the male members of my family and getting them out from underfoot." His eyes shifted to the lanky blond-haired youth running a smog check in the far end of the garage. His voice lowered a notch. "I'm raising Billy, you know."

No, he didn't know, Malcolm thought. He'd lost track of a great many things in the past three years.

Not waiting for a comment, Wally continued. "His father lit out for parts unknown when Billy was fourteen and, well, you know Velma." Wally laughed fondly, thinking of his sister. "She's got a good heart, but she even had trouble raising her hamsters when she was young. They kept dying on her. She's just not good at that sort of thing on her own."

He shrugged his shoulders. "Taking them both in seemed the only thing to do." Things had gotten a bit more hectic now that both boys were out of school. "The noise level, though, is likely to make me deaf. Nice of you to give them a place to go to in the daytime. Before you did, whenever I was home, I couldn't hear myself think."

Malcolm dismissed the older man's words. "They're earning their pay."

Wally studied Malcolm thoughtfully. He was wasting away here. The thought saddened him. "They say the same about you. And then some.'' He paused, weighing his words. He knew the wound was still tender, even after all this time. Malcolm really hadn't let it heal. ''Track could use you, and I think you could use the track.''

Malcolm knew that was what this visit was really about. To see if Wally could talk him into returning to racing. ''Not for me.''

Though his Texas twang made him sound silver tongued, Wally really knew only one way to talk. Straight. ''If it's because—''

He didn't want to hear it. If Wally was going to talk to him about burying the past and getting back to racing, he could forget about it.

''Not for me, Old Man, okay?'' he bit off curtly. Because he'd always regarded Wally with the affection he hadn't been able to give his own father, Malcolm softened. ''Besides, my reflexes aren't what they used to be. I'd be out of it in the first lap.''

Wally snorted. ''That's not what I hear.'' Malcolm looked at him, not knowing what he was getting at. ''That was a nice piece of driving you did the other week.''

Malcolm looked surprised that he knew anything about it.

Wally read his expression correctly. ''Hell, I'm not clairvoyant. If I were, I'd be a rich man now, knowing who to put my money on. It made the local edition of the papers,'' he explained.

Malcolm didn't bother reading the newspaper. To do so would be to agree to be part of the world again, and he really didn't want to be. Didn't feel as if he deserved to be. He thought that when he'd sent that annoying reporter away, that would be the end of it.

Apparently not. He wondered why Christa hadn't said anything to him about the article. It was just the kind of thing she'd bring up.

He caught himself. Since when had he become an expert on her? She was a stranger to him, just a stranger, he insisted silently. A stranger whom he'd had some emotional dealings with, but that didn't change things. Just because he'd saved her child and held her in his arms and...

Malcolm banked down his thoughts before they got the better of him.

"I don't, however," Wally was saying, "need to be clairvoyant to put my money on you."

Even if he hadn't momentarily become sidetracked, Malcolm had a feeling that he wouldn't have known what Wally was talking about.

"What's that supposed to mean?"

"You were a fighter, Malcolm."

He knew where this was going and he didn't want to hear it. Malcolm moved away, turning his attention to another car.

Wally followed, undeterred. "That was why I took you under my wing in the first place. The cock of the walk doesn't exactly welcome the new rooster on the farm unless there's something else to motivate him. Unless he sees something in that rooster that speaks to him." His broad smile went all the way up to his eyes. "You weren't just competition, boy—you had style."

"Long time ago." The dark look he gave Wally should have brought the subject to a close.

"Not that long." Wally paused, a self-deprecating smile on his lips. "An old man likes to live in his memories."

He was being toyed with, Malcolm thought, raising his eyes. But the expression on Wally's face was nostalgic. Maybe Wally wasn't doing this for effect after all. The Old Man had to be in his fifties somewhere. Maybe he was feeling the pinch of time.

"You? Old?" Malcolm scoffed softly. "Never happen."

"Yeah, it happens." Wally blew out a breath. No use in getting maudlin. That wasn't why he was here. "It's happening now. I can't go on racing much longer." He'd had a scare the last race. Losing control and spinning out had brought his own mortality before him in huge neon lights. Time to stop behaving like a cocky kid and take stock of the future. "I'm thinking of hanging up my hat at the end of the season."

Stunned, Malcolm looked at his mentor. He forgot to be defensive. The racing world wouldn't be the same without Wally Peritoni in it.

"What are you going to do?"

Wally mentally rubbed his hands together, warming to his subject. "Well, I'm not going to sit around on my duff, reading my old press clippings if that's what you mean." He watched Malcolm's eyes as he spoke, looking for a sign that he'd caught his interest. "I'm thinking of starting a defensive-driving school. You know, teaching chauffeurs of those rich dudes in the box seats how to avoid having their bosses kidnapped."

He'd be good at something like that, Malcolm thought. Especially the public-relations part. He'd have them coming out in droves.

"Sounds good," Malcolm commented.

Wally *knew* he could get Malcolm interested if he tried. "I hope so, 'cause I'm thinking of asking you to go in on it with me."

Malcolm shut the hood of the car he was working on
and stared incredulously at the older man. Out of the
corner of his eye, he could see that Jock was watching
them. From here, Jock looked as if he was holding his
breath. "You're serious."

Wally saw no reason to have to assure Malcolm of that.
They were friends. When had he ever led him on? "Yeah,
of course I'm serious. Why not?"

Malcolm gestured around the garage. They had full
work orders for the next week. Cars were lined up to be
worked on. Not to mention the fact that he had to finish
up Christa's van.

"Oh, I don't know. Maybe because I'm up to my el-
bows in work here."

Wally slipped a fatherly arm around Malcolm's
shoulders. They were almost the same height. Malcolm
only *looked* taller.

"Mechanic stuff." He saw the look that came into
Malcolm's eyes and headed it off. "Not that I'm down-
playing that. I'm the first one to love my mechanic. What
they do is the most vital part of driving a car. Your brakes
go, that's all she wrote—but you've got Billy for that."
Wally pointed to his nephew for added emphasis. Like a
coconspirator, he leaned in toward Malcolm and lowered his voice. "That boy can put an entire engine together in an hour with a blindfold on."

Malcolm laughed despite himself. There was no need
to sell him on Billy's qualifications. He'd been impressed from the first day he'd hired him. "We'll keep it
off."

Wally didn't crack a smile. "Even faster, then." He
zeroed in on his point. "But what I'm saying is that
you've got a gift."

He didn't see it as a gift. If he'd had a gift, Gloria and Sally would have still been here. Alive. "Driving fast," he scoffed.

Wally shook his head adamantly. "Driving well. Look what you did to foil that car-jacker. That's a vital service in my book. Hell, you could make a car roll over and play dead if you wanted to."

Malcolm shrugged off Wally's hand. He had work to do. "Pretty picture."

Wally wasn't about to be shrugged off. He followed Malcolm around the service area, a heat-seeking missile intent on its target.

"C'mon, whatta you say? You and me. Been a long time and I miss you, boy."

Malcolm turned to look at him. "'Boy,'" he repeated incredulously. The label didn't apply. Maybe it never had. "I haven't been a boy in what, fifteen years?"

Longer than that by Wally's estimation. "I figure you were a man the day you were born," Wally conceded, "but that's not the point."

Malcolm gave up trying to get anything done. He had trouble concentrating when he was being stalked. "What *is* the point?"

Happy to get his undivided attention, Wally went for the heart of the matter. "That you're wasting your time and talent here, buried in tires and oil filters and monkey wrenches. You gotta get out again, back into the world."

"Wally—"

But Wally wouldn't let him say no, didn't want to hear the word. He held up his hands and halted anything Malcolm was about to say. "I don't want an answer just yet. I want you to think about it." He eyed Malcolm, as if that would seal the bargain. "Promise me that you'll think about it."

Malcolm sighed. "Okay, I promise that I'll think about it." How could he say anything else?

Wally turned and beckoned for his son to join them. When he did, Wally directed Jock's attention to Malcolm. "Your boss just promised to think about my offer. See that he does, Jock."

Malcolm laughed as he shook his head. "He talks almost as much as you do," he told Wally.

Nothing could have pleased Wally more than a comparison to his son.

"Why not?" Wally hooked his arm around Jock's neck affectionately and pulled his son to him. "He's my boy. Trained him well." He looked toward Billy. "Now, *that* one," he said, purposely raising his voice, "you gotta watch all the time. Doesn't know a piston from a spark plug, but I guess, with my blood in him, he'll get the hang of it by and by."

Hearing, Billy flashed a grin at his uncle. He waved with the end of a wrench before resuming his work.

"Works all the time, does he?" Wally asked, releasing Jock. Malcolm nodded. "Reminds me of you." Well, his mission had been pushed as far as it could go for the moment. "So, you'll think about it?"

There was only one way to get rid of Wally and that was to agree with everything he said. "I'll think about it."

Malcolm never said what he didn't mean. That was one of the things Wally liked about him. For the time being, Wally was satisfied.

"Good." He launched into the next point on his agenda. "Now then, how about coming over to the house for dinner one night? Velma might not know much about raising a kid, but she's still one hell of a cook. You're probably just living on sandwiches, like the old days."

The old days were before he'd gotten married. Before things had changed. He wasn't ready to take that step yet, to socialize with people from the world he'd once known before the accident.

"I—"

Wally just wasn't going to allow him to get in a word edgewise. "Bring the lady along."

"Lady?" he repeated, mystified.

"The one whose van you've been working on."

Malcolm's look of surprise melted as he shifted his eyes toward Jock. Wally followed his gaze and rode to his son's defense. "Hell, there're no secrets in my family. I pump him for information every time I talk to him. Otherwise, what good is he?" His eyes narrowed on Malcolm. "Dinner?"

"Maybe." That was as far as he planned to commit himself.

Wally nodded, deciphering the message. He had no intentions of giving up. "I'll call you."

Malcolm knew that he could put money on that. Affection filtered into his voice. "You are a pain, Old Man, you know that?"

The laugh was deep and hearty, shaking the small belly Wally had acquired from too many beers at too many parties.

"Never said I wasn't." Turning, he was about to leave when he let out a low, appreciative whistle. There was a long-legged blonde approaching. The description matched what his son had told him. "That one yours, boy?"

Before Malcolm could make the denial, Jock identified Christa.

"That's the lady I was telling you about, Dad. The one whose van Malcolm's fixing."

The man still had classy taste, Wally thought as he watched the woman walk toward them. She moved like poetry through a world accustomed to mundane words. Dressed in white shorts and low-heeled mules that set off her legs to their advantage—not that he thought they could possibly be set to a *dis*advantage—she had on a tank top that looked as if it had been ordered directly from heaven.

Renewed respect entered his eyes as he looked at Malcolm. "My, oh my, her legs do go all the way up, don't they?"

Suddenly, Malcolm was busy again. "Looks that way."

"Looks?" Wally's eyes narrowed as he turned toward Malcolm. He had to be misunderstanding this. "You mean you and the lady haven't..." His voice trailed off, but there was no mistaking the meaning behind them.

"No, we haven't," Malcolm fairly growled, warning Wally off as Christa came closer.

Damn, why did she have to pick now to come here? And what was she doing here, anyway? He'd already told her that he would see her tonight. Did it have anything to do with the car-jacker's arraignment? He suddenly remembered that it was today.

Pity filled Wally's bright blue eyes. "Never thought of you as being backward, boy." The mournful look gave him a hangdog expression. "Looks like you've lost more than your edge, festering here in this grease pit."

"I haven't been—" The protest never had a chance to be heard. As Malcolm watched, thunderstruck, Wally crossed to Christa.

Wally captured Christa's hand in his, shaking it before she had a chance to pull away. "Hi, my name's Wally Peritoni."

Bemused, she looked at Malcolm for an explanation. He was standing directly behind the older man, scowling at him. She'd just seen the two of them talking.

"I'm a friend of Malcolm's from his racing days," Wally explained smoothly. "I'm having a little dinner at my house tomorrow night. You free?"

Talk about someone working fast . . . Christa couldn't picture the two men as friends. This Wally person talked as fast as Malcolm spoke slow.

"Well, I—"

"Because Malcolm here needs a date, but he's too shy to say anything. I thought I'd help him out. How about it, little lady, you game on making two men happy?"

As far as snow jobs went, she was in the middle of a Texas blizzard. And enjoying herself immensely. "That all depends on what's involved."

Wally laughed, tickled. "I like her, Mal, I surely do." He held her hand a moment longer. "Twenty years ago, I might've given ol' Malcolm a run for his money over you. Of course, twenty years ago, you were probably just a baby." He chuckled to himself, charming Christa. "Time does have a way of getting away from you. Nothing's involved except eating, little darlin'," he finally answered her. "And talking—if I let you get in a word."

That, she could readily believe.

Still holding her hand, Wally glanced over his shoulder at his son and nephew. "I guess it being a special occasion and all, we'll let you two eat at the table."

"What special occasion?" Christa asked.

His eyes seemed to twinkle as he looked at her. "Why, you're coming to dinner, of course." He released her hand. "Gotta go. See you tomorrow." He was already hurrying away. "Malcolm'll tell you where I live—if he hasn't forgotten."

Christa let out a long breath as she watched Wally stride away.

Malcolm could easily guess what she was thinking. He crossed to her. "He lays it on a little thick." He didn't want her to feel obligated because Wally was his friend. "You don't have to go."

She turned so quickly, her hair whipped along his bare arm. "Oh, no, I'd like to go. Providing that you want me to."

She wasn't going to run her car down his track. "I don't have anything to say about it."

He was shying away again. Why wasn't she surprised? "Well, you do have the address," she countered.

Malcolm strode back to the work area and the car he'd abandoned. "I can give you that."

Christa glanced at the sign prohibiting her entry as she followed him to the lift. "You could also give me a ride, since you've got all four of my tires off the van."

That situation would be easily remedied. "I'll be finished working on the brakes tonight."

Was he saying he wasn't going? "Does that mean you won't give me a ride? I think he's counting on us arriving together."

He knew the way Wally operated. The man wasn't satisfied until he had everything his way. But not this time. That included going in with the Old Man on the school. All Malcolm wanted was to be left alone.

"He's counting on a lot of things, but he doesn't always have to have his way."

"Who *is* he?"

He supposed there was no harm in telling her. It was a matter of record.

He got into the car and turned on the engine. It hummed. "Someone who taught me everything I know about racing. Jock's father." He nodded at the gangly youth.

Christa leaned into the car window. "He seemed nice." She curbed the urge to smooth her fingers over his frown. Curbed the urge to touch his face just to feel his skin. He would only misconstrue it.

Or construe it correctly, she amended ruefully.

"So," she said, clearing her throat, taking a step back as he got out again. "Are we going to his dinner party?"

In his mind, he'd already turned down the invitation for both of them. The look on her face had him rethinking his decision. "You don't mind going?"

"Mind?" Her face lit up. "I think it would be fun."

He remembered the old days and parties that went on until dawn and longer. Gloria had never liked them. She'd opted for a quiet life. A little quieter than he'd liked. "I wouldn't go that far—the Old Man can get a little rowdy at times."

Christa laughed. Was that all that was stopping him from taking her? "I grew up with a father and two older brothers. Rowdy doesn't scare me."

There was something about the way she said it that caught his attention. The question seemed to come on its own. "What does scare you, Christa?"

That was easy. "Being shut out."

The moment, and the meaning, hung between them, isolating them from everything around them.

He looked away first. "Yeah, well, sometimes that can't be helped."

She refused to believe that. "Yes, it can. It can always be helped."

The look in his eyes was flinty. "Maybe the hinges on the door are rusted shut."

"They can always be oiled. WD-40 does wonders. All you've got to do is want it to work." Walking around him so that she could face him, she met his eyes. "Ways can be found."

For a single moment, he felt the urge to take her into his arms, to kiss her so that both their heads spun. So that there wasn't a trace of oxygen left between them. But that was purely irrational, and he wasn't irrational. Just irritated. And tired.

"Did you walk here again?"

He was changing the subject on her, but she was growing accustomed to that.

"No, my dad dropped me off. He and Robin are in the florist shop—buying flowers."

He went to the workbench and wrote something down on the last work order. "Seems like the thing to do in a florist shop." Hanging the paper up on a nail, he slipped the key ring over it.

The man was impossible. "Don't you want to know why?"

Malcolm took down another order and looked it over quickly. "I figure you'll tell me if you want me to know."

She sighed. There probably wasn't a curious bone in his body. "It's for June, the woman he went out with the day you rescued Robin," she explained quickly. She followed him out to the lot, where the next car was parked. "I think they've got a thing going." Christa grinned, pleased.

Malcolm stopped and turned to her. Her initial phrase rang in his ears. "Are you going to continue to mark time that way, relating it to the day I 'rescued Robin'?"

She saw that it irritated him and had no idea why. "Yes."

"Why?"

"Because that was the day my life started again." In more ways that one, she thought. "Anyway, I thought I'd just stop and say hi before I did some shopping." She nodded at the stationery store that was next to the doughnut shop.

A brow quirked. "More shopping?"

Christa laughed at his expression. "Just for decorations. Robin's party's Saturday," she reminded him.

He knew she was waiting for him to say that he'd be there, but he didn't know if he would be. Common sense told him not to go. His emotions were saying something else. He'd have to thrash it out later.

"Yeah, I know. Look, I've got a lot of work to do. I'll see you later." With that, he got into the black sedan and started it up.

She was being dismissed, Christa thought, watching Malcolm drive the car onto the lift. With a wave of her hand, she walked toward the stationery store.

One step at a time, she told herself. She couldn't hurry him any more than that. Only one step at a time.

She just really wished the steps were a little bigger than they were.

Chapter Eleven

"I wasn't sure if you were going to show up."

Christa opened the door farther, stepping back to admit Malcolm. She'd been holding her breath ever since he'd told her last night that he'd be by today at six to pick her up for Wally's dinner party.

He hadn't been sure he'd show up, either. He'd wavered back and forth half a dozen times, telling himself he was only getting in deeper where he shouldn't be.

Someplace he couldn't seem to help himself being.

Malcolm shrugged as Christa closed the door behind him. "I had no choice. You don't know the Old Man. If we don't show up, he'll continue calling me every day until I finally turn up at his dinner table. Once he's made up his mind about something, that's it. I thought I'd save myself a headache."

He looked around. She'd done something different to the room, he mused. Then he realized what it was. The listing coffee table had been replaced by one that looked sturdier. She was settling in.

Turning, he looked at Christa. She was wearing her hair up in a twist, but a few curls had worked their way loose. He felt the urge to pull the pins out and watch it all tumble down her back. To bury his face in it.

He stepped back, from her and his thoughts. "I didn't see the Jaguar when I pulled up."

"My father's not here yet. You're early." That had surprised her. But then, everything about the man surprised her. Suddenly feeling fidgety, she gestured toward the kitchen. "Would you like something to drink?"

"No, I'm fine." He glanced down. She was barefoot. He guessed that she wasn't planning to spend the evening that way. "Why don't you finish getting ready?"

Feeling some definitely schoolgirl sensations sliding through her, she nodded and withdrew. It was silly, after having associated with the man on a daily basis, to suddenly feel like this just because they were officially going out. It wasn't as if this was a date. It was an evening out. There was a world of difference between an evening out and a date.

No, there wasn't.

She grinned at him. They were actually, finally, going out on a date. "I'll be just a minute longer."

Glancing over her shoulder, she saw him sit down on one of the lawn chairs. Those would be replaced next, she vowed. Something wide and accommodating, where he could feel comfortable. Right now, he was sitting on the edge of the chair as if he expected to shoot out of the room at a moment's notice.

When was he going to feel at ease? she wondered. Maybe being around his friend would help. She could only hope.

Clutching a fistful of crayons and what looked to be a much-dragged-about coloring book, Robin made her entrance from the dining alcove and presented herself to Malcolm.

Warmth spread through him instantly. "Hi, Robin. Found any more fountains to fall into?"

She gave him an uncomprehending, blank stare, blinked her huge blue eyes and then thrust the book and crayons at him. "Ka-lor."

As lost as she had been when he'd asked her about the fountain, Malcolm looked at the crayons. She was obviously waiting for a response from him. "Yes, they certainly are."

Impatience puckered the small oval face, and she frowned. Once again, Robin pushed the crayons at him. He had to move back to avoid being indelibly marked. At least by the crayons. He had a feeling that it might be too late to avoid it in the absolute sense.

"Ka-lor," Robin insisted again.

What was she saying to him? He glanced at the cover of the coloring book, hoping to get a clue. The drawing of a storybook didn't help.

Malcolm shook his head, helpless. "I don't—"

"*Ka-lor,*" she announced a third time. She waved her crayons for emphasis. Then stuck out her lower lip and added, "Peas?"

"Peas? Oh, you mean 'please,' don't you?" he corrected absently. What was she saying? "It's like trying to communicate with an alien. A very pretty alien, mind you." He slid his finger down the tip of her nose, and Robin giggled. "But an alien nonetheless. Bet your mother can't wait until you can really talk." He glanced over his shoulder toward the hall where Christa had disappeared. "Then the rest of the world won't be able to get in a word edgewise, except maybe for the Old Man."

"Ka-lor?" This time, the word was uttered mournfully.

Since she was butting the crayons against his chest, Malcolm took them from her. As frustrated as she was, Malcolm played the single word over and over again in his head.

And then it dawned on him. It was clear as a bell, now that he realized what she was saying. "You want me to color, don't you?"

As triumphant as if she'd just scaled a tall peak, the silky head bobbed up and down with abandoned glee.

"Ka-lor!" she squealed, pointing to the coloring book, which was now on the floor.

"I'm not much good at this," he warned her. Glancing at the opened page, he saw the scribbled blue lines that crisscrossed all over Miss Muffett's face, trapping her, as well as the spider, in a blue web. "Apparently, neither are you."

She was standing there, watching him with those blue eyes of hers, looking as if she was absorbing every word he said.

"Good trick," he commented. "Cultivate it. Men love it when you listen to them. They don't have to know you don't understand a word they're saying."

"Ka-lor?"

He laughed. "Two years old and a one-track mind already. You're going to go far, Robin." He surrendered. "All right, 'color.'" Malcolm looked around for someplace to lean on. He decided not to test the integrity of the coffee table, just in case. "I've got an idea," he told Robin. "Why don't we try doing this together?"

Which was the way Christa found them.

Malcolm was sitting on the floor with Robin propped up between his legs. He was holding her hand in his and guiding the stubby fingers along the picture of a school house.

"There, there you go. See, you're getting the hang of it," he encouraged. "If you learn how to stay within the lines, you're going to wow them in preschool."

Touched beyond words, Christa covered her mouth with her hands and blinked back a tear that suddenly, insistently, had materialized.

She would have been content just to stand there, watching them, for the rest of the evening. But the doorbell cut the scene short for her.

Malcolm looked up when he heard the bell. Chagrined, he realized that Christa had been watching them. He felt uncomfortable again, as if he'd been caught slipping into a role he had no business playing.

"What?"

Why didn't he want her to see this softer side of him? She'd already suspected as much after he'd changed Robin at the mall.

Christa smiled at him. "You look so natural."

He shrugged off her words as if they were an annoying drizzle. Gathering Robin to him, he moved her and her crayons aside, then rose to his feet. The doorbell rang again. "Don't you think you'd better answer that?"

Coming to, Christa flushed. "Right."

When she opened the door, Jonas stood there, carefully surveying the scene.

"I was beginning to think you'd changed your mind." Jonas nodded a greeting at Malcolm, then turned his attention to Robin. "So, how's my favorite girl?" Squatting, he opened his arms to her.

There was a moment's hesitation as Robin looked first at her grandfather, then Malcolm, before flying into the old man's outstretched arms.

"I'm raising a femme fatale," Christa murmured with a shake of her head.

Without cracking a smile, Malcolm responded, "Everyone's got to be something." But he could feel a smile in his soul as he placed a hand on Christa's arm and guided her out the door.

He could damn well feel one, he thought. And that was both good and bad.

Malcolm had obeyed the summons, coming to Wally's home out of a sense of obligation. Also a sense of survival. What he'd told Christa earlier was true. Once he'd made up his mind to see Malcolm sitting at his table, Wally would go on calling and nudging until he made it happen.

It was because of Wally that Malcolm had discovered and moved to Bedford to begin with. Wally had settled in the then-just-forming college town twenty-five years ago. When Malcolm had begun looking around for a place to relocate his family, Wally had touted Bedford as the "best little city in the country." At forty-five thousand, it wasn't all that little anymore, but it was still a good place to raise a family, Malcolm mused.

If a man had a family to raise.

Malcolm had a better time at dinner than he had thought possible, given his frame of mind. Wally's sister Velma was the perfect hostess. Malcolm had met her several times at the track and had taken an immediate liking to her. Like her brother, she was a comfortable person to talk to. She made people feel instantly at home, no matter what the circumstances.

And there was just enough nostalgia at the table to make him smile and not enough to make him ache.

That came about because of Christa.

Wally regaled Christa with story after story about Malcolm's racing career. The spotlight widened every so often to include him, as well. Unlike his son and nephew, who had heard it all countless times, Christa was a fresh audience and Wally loved it.

So did she.

"You're indulging an old man," he told her, laughing after he'd finished one long story he was particularly fond of.

His eyes certainly didn't sparkle like an old man's, Christa thought. She would be willing to bet that there was a great deal of life left in Wally Peritoni.

"No, I love it, really. I love hearing all about your career."

She was unaware that the glance she gave Malcolm had love written all over it. But Wally was quick to pick it up.

'Bout time, he thought.

Christa smiled ruefully but she made no apologies. "I guess I never outgrew my need for stories."

Laughing again, Wally rubbed his hands together. "Well then, darlin', I could keep you glued to your seat until the rooster crows in the morning." His smile was wide as he looked at Malcolm. "Knew I liked this little lady right from the start."

The hour was late. They'd already stayed far longer than Malcolm had initially anticipated. "Some roosters have to get up early in the morning." He rose.

Squinty gray eyes shifted to the clock on the mantelpiece. It was almost eleven. "Sorry, forgot about the time." He unfolded his lanky body from the recliner and rose to join them. "Not like the old days, eh? When there weren't any watches except the ones they clocked us with at the track.''

Malcolm's lips curved slightly. He remembered. Those were the wilder days, the days where the only restrictions on him were the ones he'd imposed of his own free will. Not the ones that shackled him now.

He paused, taking a long hard look at Wally. The Old Man represented the best of his times. But all that was neatly packed away now.

"We'd better be leaving," Christa agreed. Her father had to be getting tired by now. "Much as I hate to."

"Then you'll be sure to come back now, hear?" Wally drawled the instruction. He hated giving up his audience.

"I'd like that," Christa told him. She stole a glance at Malcolm, but his face was unreadable.

They said their goodbyes to Jock, Billy and Velma. Wally walked them to the door. "You been thinking about what I said?" he asked Malcolm.

Malcolm had wondered when he'd get around to that. He had been trying *not* to think of what Wally had said. "Yes."

Wally eyed him, trying to mentally force him to agree. "And?"

Malcolm took Christa's arm, urging her outside. "And I'm still thinking."

It wasn't good enough for Wally. Knowing he needed help, he enlisted reinforcements and shifted his line of attack to Christa.

"You get him to agree, little darlin'. It'd be the best thing in the world for him."

Knowing she wasn't going to get any information out of Malcolm, she looked at Wally. "Agree to what?"

"Never mind," Malcolm said tersely.

Wally disregarded the warning. He took hold of Christa's other arm, detaining her. "Opening up a defensive-driving school with me. He'd be doing people a service, teaching them to drive like him."

Christa felt like a wishbone, being pulled between the two men.

Malcolm's expression darkened so that she hardly recognized him. "Yeah, a real service," he said.

"Can't you get it through your damn-fool head once and for all that it wasn't your fault?" Wally demanded.

Malcolm didn't answer. Instead, he commandeered Christa and began walking to his car. "Good night, Old Man. Thanks for the hospitality."

"It wasn't your fault," Wally insisted, calling after Malcolm's retreating back.

Christa waited until she was in the car before she asked, "What did he mean, it wasn't your fault?"

He'd entertained the vague hope that she'd let the matter drop. He should have known better. "Nothing, he was just talking."

Gunning the engine, Malcolm took off. Then, as if silently chiding himself, he eased his foot off the accelerator.

Christa tried to read his expression and got nowhere. "About what?" she pressed. "The accident?"

He didn't look at her. "I don't want to talk about it."

She wasn't going to let him put her off any longer. She heard things in his voice that he wasn't saying aloud. "Yes, you do."

Malcolm's hands tightened on the wheel as he struggled to hold on to his temper. "Don't tell me what I want."

Maybe she should have backed away, but she couldn't. Not anymore. "We can't keep skirting around it. Things aren't going to go forward for you, or for us, until you bring this thing that's eating away at you out into the open.''

Things had been fine until she'd come into his life. He'd resigned himself to the living hell he was in. Why did she have come barging in to remind him of the daylight that still existed?

His mouth hardened. ''What makes you think I want things to go forward for us?''

That hurt. For a moment, she fell silent as all the air left her lungs. But this was bigger than just her hurt feelings. This was about him. About saving another human being.

She found her tongue. ''What makes me think you want things to go forward for us?'' she echoed. ''The way you kiss me. The way you look at me sometimes. The way you looked with Robin tonight.'' He wasn't budging. Exasperated, she added, ''The way you spent almost two weeks fixing a van that you could've had towed to your place and finished up in five days. Maybe six.''

She was hitting too close to home, making him admit things to himself he didn't want to admit. ''Repairs became complicated, and you didn't have money for towing, remember?''

''You could've overridden that. You gloss over everything else that you don't want to pay attention to.'' She bit back her anger. He had to talk to her. He *had* to. ''Tell me, Malcolm, tell me what happened, once and for all. Please.''

The silence separated them, pushing them each into a small corner on opposite ends of the car and slamming an invisible door.

Finally, he blew out a long breath, exhaling with it the final bit of his reserve.

"I didn't see the truck coming." As he spoke, it began to happen all over again in his mind's eye. He was there, reliving it, feeling the helplessness as it ate away at his soul. "We were arguing and I didn't see the truck coming."

When he paused, she pressed. "Arguing?"

"Arguing. About racing." It was so ironic—what had attracted Gloria to him in the first place became such a sore point after they were married. After Sally came. "It wasn't a new argument, just more heated this time. Gloria didn't want me to go on taking risks. She said I was a father now and had responsibilities to live up to. That I had to stop behaving like a selfish little boy and take a man's job. She wanted me to go to work for her father." There was no humor in the smile on his lips. "He manufactured sports equipment. I couldn't see myself being a salesman for the rest of my life.

"So I argued with her. Racing was the only thing I knew. The only thing I felt I was good at. The only thing, I shouted at her, that I loved." Tears threatened to close his throat as he remembered the horror and the guilt. And the emptiness. "When I woke up, that was all I had left. Racing. And I walked away from it. Because that was the last thing she'd asked of me. I..." His voice trailed off.

Christa felt as if her own heart was breaking. "Go on," she urged quietly.

He let out a shaky breath. He didn't want to continue, but she was right. He had to get it out. Inside, it was festering like a cancer, eating him up alive.

"I took my eyes off the road for one second, just one damn, lousy second. The driver in the truck was drunk. He'd fallen asleep at the wheel. It swerved into mine.'' Malcolm bit down lips that were dry. ''I tried to avoid it, but it was too late.''

He could see it all now, just as it had happened then. The headlights coming at him, Gloria screaming. The sickening crunch of metal against metal as he'd tried frantically to steer them out of the way.

''Sally and Gloria were killed instantly. So was the other driver. The police said it was a miracle I was alive. Some miracle.'' He had wanted to die with them. Because he couldn't save them from being killed.

Christa placed a hand on his arm, a hand he hardly felt. ''It wasn't your fault.''

''Yes, it was,'' he shot back fiercely. ''I was a trained professional, a skilled driver. I should have been able to—''

''To what? Make the car fly? You're not God,'' Christa insisted. She saw the way his jaw hardened. She had to get through to him. ''Pull over.''

They were traveling down a lonely stretch of land. One of the last pieces of farmland left in Bedford was on their left, and a grove of eucalyptus trees was on their right.

''What?''

''Pull over,'' Christa repeated. ''Right there.'' She pointed to the side. Just up ahead was a lamppost, casting a yellow-white light that pooled on the paved road. It looked like a spotlight.

He began to protest, then shrugged and did as she instructed. ''All right. Now what?''

''Now you'll listen to me.'' Her voice was quiet but firm. ''It wasn't your fault. The man was drunk, he ran into you.''

What did she know? She wasn't there. ''If I wasn't arguing with Gloria—''

No one could ever second-guess fate. "You still might not have seen him coming."

Shifting, Malcolm glared at her. "So what are you saying, that I still would have killed them?"

So that was it; that was the burden he carried with him. "You didn't kill them, Malcolm. You tried to save them and you couldn't. You tried to save Robin and you could." Trying to make him listen, she took his hands in hers and held on tightly. "Not everything is in your hands, Malcolm. You can only try your best. The rest gets taken care of without your say-so."

She wasn't reaching him, she thought in despair. She could see it in his eyes.

"Now I'm very, very sorry you lost your wife and daughter, but I am very, very happy you were there to save mine." A tear rolled down her cheek. She ignored it. "And I would like you to be there to teach her how to color in the lines before she gets into preschool. And I'd like you there to hold me and make me feel safe." Christa swallowed the other tears that threatened to come. Maybe it was admitting too much, but she couldn't help herself. "You do, you know. You make me feel very safe."

"Then you're very foolish," he whispered.

Malcolm slipped his hands from hers and slid them along her face, burying his fingers in her hair. He kissed her then, kissed her because his emotions were raw and exposed, kissed her because he had to, wanted to. Was compelled to.

He kissed her in hopes that all the broken pieces within him would somehow be joined together to form a whole.

He kissed her, praying that he could forget.

She felt the desperation on his lips, in his soul. Felt it and tried very hard to help it heal. But she knew it wasn't going to be done in a moment or in a week. It could only be done a little at a time.

She fervently hoped that she'd said enough to make it begin.

Malcolm drew back, his heart drumming madly in his ears the way it always did at the beginning of a race. But this wasn't a race. This was an interlude. Nothing else.

"Very foolish," he repeated. Shifting around in his seat, he started the car again. "I'd better get you home."

The way he said it, she knew it was her home, not his, they were driving to. And that he would be leaving her at the door.

The same door was slamming shut again, harder this time than before. She sighed quietly and sat back in her seat, trying not to let the tears come.

Chapter Twelve

Christa tried to not let it bother her. After all, Malcolm had never actually given her a definite commitment. He hadn't come out and said he was coming to the party in so many words. It was just something she'd inferred.

Something she'd hoped.

She should have suspected that he wouldn't show, though. The van was in running order, and she hadn't seen him in three days.

For Robin's sake, she was so cheerful that it hurt.

It did hurt.

It hurt that Malcolm could just walk away without a word. That he couldn't even call to tell her he wasn't going to come to Robin's birthday party.

With a little more vigor than was called for, Christa cleaned up the floor, which was littered with shredded wrapping paper. She shoved the trash into a huge garbage bag while her father showed Robin how to make music on the small portable keyboard June had given the little girl.

Who the hell needed Malcolm, anyway?

She did, damn it.

In an incredibly short amount of time, she'd grown to really need him. It wasn't like her, this feeling she was carrying around. She had never needed anyone, not to this degree. Not even Jim.

Ever since she could remember, there had always been a small part of herself that she'd managed to hold in reserve, like a spare generator to fall back on when the main one failed.

But this time, there didn't seem to be any extra energy supply available. She was emotionally spent. She'd already given everything to him that she had to give.

The package, obviously, had been returned, unused— unopened and marked Return To Sender.

Rising to her feet, Christa yanked the two ends of the garbage bag closed. These things happened, she told herself.

It didn't help.

"Nice party," Tyler commented as he cut another small piece of cake for himself.

The cake was sitting in the center of a dining table he, his father and brother had surprised Christa with. A belated housewarming gift. She'd christened it with her mother's tablecloth. There was a feeling of closeness that pervaded the house. She wanted Malcolm to feel a part of it. To *be* a part of it.

Christa ran her hand along the table now and smiled in response. It was her brother's third piece of cake. She'd held back cutting into the cake as long as possible, without telling the others why. She had a feeling they suspected anyway.

"Too bad she won't remember it when she grows up," Christa murmured.

In reply, she suddenly found herself the focus of Ethan's video camera. It was her brother's latest toy, and he was taping everything that moved. Robin's birthday party seemed to be the perfect excuse for him to play Steven Spielberg.

"She can always watch it on tape." Ethan zoomed in on her, only to have Christa avert her face. "C'mon, Christa, smile. I want to capture you for posterity."

Sensitive to the look in Christa's eyes, Tyler placed himself between his sister and Ethan's lens. "Back off, Ethan. Can't you see that she doesn't want to be 'captured'?"

"That's because she already has been," Jonas interjected. He placed the two empty plates he was carrying onto the table. Glancing at his daughter as he cut a piece for himself and one for June, he asked, "Speaking of which, where is he?"

"Whom," Christa corrected automatically.

Jonas waved an impatient hand. "Which, whom, you know what I mean. Where the hell is he?"

Tyler flashed his father a silencing look that was ignored.

Christa moved past Jonas. She could feign cheerfulness, but she couldn't withstand an interrogation. Not when she didn't have any of the answers herself. "He couldn't make it."

Jonas pivoted on his heel so that he faced her again. "Why?"

Tyler took his father's arm and directed him to the plates of cake. "Dad, I think June wants her cake before it gets stale."

Jonas opened his mouth to say something, then just shrugged and crossed to June.

Christa let out a long breath, then raised her eyes to Tyler. ''Thanks.''

They hardly looked like each other, except when they grinned. Then the family resemblance was evident.

''Hey, what are big brothers for?'' So saying, he hooked an arm through Ethan's and pulled him away. ''Why don't you take a few more dozen feet of film of Robin? After all, it's her birthday, not Christa's.''

''Yeah, but—'' Ethan's protest was cut short by the doorbell.

Christa and Tyler exchanged glances. There was no missing the hopeful look that had risen to her eyes.

Tyler crossed his fingers before him so that only Christa could see.

This was ridiculous. She was a grown woman, for heaven's sake. Why was her heart suddenly hammering like a fire-alarm system gone berserk?

She was a grown woman who had fallen in love. Hard. Slowly drawing in a breath to steady her jangled nerves, Christa went to open the door.

Yes!

The single word drummed through her brain like the triumphant roar of a crowd when the winning home run was hit at the bottom of the ninth with two outs.

Malcolm was standing on her front step, a gaily wrapped package in his hands and a Big Wheel positioned at his feet. There was a big red bow affixed to each one of the handlebars. The multicolored streamers were waving softly in the wind.

Now that he'd come, he felt awkward. Uncustomarily shy. He had faced huge, cheering crowds and bars teeming with celebrating racing fans and friends and had embraced both. Yet a small room full of people, her people, made him feel awkward.

Maybe he shouldn't have come.

No, he should have, he thought. This was the next logical step. He'd already called Wally and told him that he was going to go in on the driving school with him. He'd taken himself out of the netherworld he'd existed in. Now he had to close the door behind him.

Malcolm glanced down at the toy. "Um, it took me longer to put this thing together than I estimated. You'd think a mechanic could slap the pieces together with his eyes shut, but—"

Impulsively, she touched her lips to his, cutting his explanation short. "It doesn't matter now, Malcolm. You're here."

Malcolm looked about the room as she pulled him inside. "The party's not over yet." He'd entertained the faint hope that maybe it would be by now.

"Almost," she said.

Had he purposely been late to avoid the others? Or was it her he'd tried to avoid and not succeeded? That didn't matter, either, she told herself. He was here.

"And here's the birthday girl," she announced as Robin made a beeline for them.

"Bi-w'ee!" The words burst from Robin's lips as she ran over to the toy. Her eyes looked as if they were going to pop out of her head.

Belatedly, it registered. Malcolm had arrived bearing the toy that she had burned up the phone wires searching for. The three Toylands in her area all professed that their supply had been depleted and wouldn't be replenished until the beginning of the next month. All the other, smaller toy stores gave her the same answer. For some reason, there was a dearth of Big Wheel toys.

She stared down at the toy. "Where did you get this?"

He didn't want to tell her that he'd combed first Orange County and then L.A. for it. At least, not in front of witnesses.

"In a toy store," he answered vaguely.

She knew how to read him and didn't press. It was enough to know that he must have gone through one hell of a search to find this. And he'd done it for Robin.

"Well, you can see that you've really made her day." Christa nodded at the gift he still had tucked under his arm. "What's that?"

"Just something else I picked up for her." Malcolm moved aside as Robin tested out her vehicle. He liked his shins unbruised. Turning to Christa, he handed her the box. "You might as well open it. She seems to be busy."

"Here, let your old uncle the motorcycle cop show you how to mount one." Ethan grasped Robin by the waist and deposited her on the seat.

Christa rolled her eyes at Ethan's words before carefully unwrapping the other box Malcolm brought.

Her breath caught in her throat as she stared, then raised questioning eyes to his face. Beneath the ivory tissue paper was the red velvet dress from Tots 'n' Togs. The dress he'd told her was far too impractical to buy.

"You bought it," she whispered.

"Thought it the best way, seeing as how you have three policemen in the family who might not be very understanding if I stole it."

"Hey, don't look at me," Jonas quipped. "I'm retired. I'm just a private citizen now. You can do whatever the hell you want." He chuckled under his breath as he shared something in private with June.

"But why?" Christa asked Malcolm. He'd made the purchase sound so frivolous, so foolish, that she had given up thinking about it.

He hadn't thought that he'd have to explain his actions to her. He'd assumed she'd thank him and that would be that. He was beginning to see that nothing was ever just *that* with Christa.

Malcolm shrugged in reply. "A girl's got to get dressed up once in a while. Besides, I owed her an outfit after I let hers get drenched."

"It wasn't ruined," she corrected gently.

Malcolm placed a finger to her lips. "Don't quibble. Just take it."

Her smile was beginning to curl all through her, rising from her toes on up. Taking Malcolm by the hand, she turned toward the rear of the house.

"If you'll excuse me," she said to the others, weaving her way to the patio, "I have something to take care of."

Malcolm was aware that the others were looking at them with knowing smiles—except for Robin, who was too busy making noise and tearing around the living room on her new mode of transportation.

"What's this all about?" Malcolm addressed the question to the back of Christa's head.

Christa didn't answer until she had him where she wanted him: on the patio. Sliding the glass door closed behind them, she turned, her body brushing against his in the small enclosure.

Feeling her body whisper along his just reminded him how useless all the arguments he'd tried to use to keep from coming here had been.

Her smile warmed him. "I just wanted to say thank you in private. I didn't think you'd like a public display of gratitude, even if it is my family."

She was beginning to understand him, he thought. Or maybe she'd always understood, and it was he who hadn't. "Well, I'm waiting."

The smile turned into a impish grin. "Really?"

"Really."

Talk about an about-face. Christa stood on her toes and sealed her mouth to his. It was like a plug entering a socket. Instant electricity went flowing through her. Through him.

The fit felt so right.

His body, heating, leaned into hers as he took her into his arms. His mouth made love to her, making silent promises he intended to keep.

He tasted her moan in his mouth and knew that he hadn't blown it by keeping away. He'd been afraid of that, afraid that she would accuse him of playing games and send him packing. The only game he knew how to play was for keeps. He had needed the time to sort out his thoughts and the feelings that were breaking free. Time to sort them out and put the guilt aside once and for all. What he felt for Christa had given him the strength to accept what he couldn't change.

He drew his head back and looked into her eyes. "Well, that was good for starters," he told her.

There was something different about him, more relaxed, something more— She didn't know. It didn't have a name. It just was.

"We could work on a continuance," she offered.

"I'd like that." He fitted his arms comfortably about her waist. "I wasn't late because I had trouble putting that thing together, you know."

"I know." And she did. But she had allowed him his excuse if it had made him feel better.

Of course she knew. She knew everything. Especially the way to his heart. "I was giving myself one last chance to back out."

She wasn't going to ask why. She could guess. It didn't matter. "Failed, huh?"

He nodded. "Miserably."

"Are you?" She searched his face. "Are you miserable?"

"No, I'm not." His hands tightened around her. "Not anymore. You cracked the darkness, Christa. The black shell I'd crawled into. I can't stay there anymore." He kissed her face, one tiny kiss at a time. He could feel her excitement. Feel his own as it grew. "Spears of daylight keep coming in. Rays of sunshine. And they all have your name on it. Yours and Robin's."

If her heart hammered any harder, it was going to fall out. "Speaking for both of us, that makes us very happy." Suddenly, she remembered. "Oh, I have a gift for you, too."

A gift? Why would she buy him anything? She'd already given him the greatest gift a man could hope for. His soul.

"It's not my birthday." But maybe in a way, it was. The birth of the rest of his life.

He hoped.

She laughed, shaking her head as she opened the storage unit. With all the gifts spread out in the living room, it was now empty, except for the one wrapped gift she'd placed inside. "You don't have to have an occasion, or a reason, to buy a gift. Here."

He made quick work of the wrapping paper, feeling like a kid for perhaps the first time. She'd done that for him, too.

He was holding the model of the race car he'd seen in the toy store. Surprised, Malcolm looked into her face.

She couldn't read his expression. Did he like it? Or had she just made a fool of herself? "You've given me so much, I just wanted to give you something, and I didn't know what."

He laid the box down. He couldn't hold it and her at the same time. Malcolm drew her back into his arms.

"You already did. You gave me back my life. Being around you and Robin makes me happy. I felt guilty about that, guilty that I was drawn to someone else, that I wanted another family. But you were right. It wasn't my fault." He'd gone over and over it in his mind the past few days, rather than shutting it out the way he'd done these past few years. It made him aware of things, things he had no control over. "I really did everything I could."

Safe in the haven of his arms, she raised her eyes to meet his. "I know."

What had he ever done to deserve to get so lucky twice? "I need you, Christa, you and Robin. I'm a family man without a family, which leaves me with a vacancy. Do you want to fill the position?"

She cocked her head and regarded him thoughtfully. "That all depends."

He wasn't aware that he had stopped breathing, but she was. "On what?"

"Do you love me?"

Malcolm stared at her, dumbfounded. "Oh course I love you. I wouldn't be asking you to marry me if I didn't."

Her eyes coaxed him. "Then say it."

"Say what?"

"That you love me."

Nothing pleased him more. "I love you. I love you, Christa, and I want you to marry me. Okay?"

"Very okay." She lifted her mouth to his to show him just *how* okay it was.

Jonas knocked on the inside of the sliding glass door. Too content to feel self-conscious, they merely looked at him.

"You two get lost out here?" As the question came out, he saw the embrace he'd interrupted. "Never mind." Turning on his heel, he waved a dismissive hand in their direction, pretending that he'd never seen them. "Carry on."

Which they did.

Neither one noticed the tiny figure beyond the glass, who clapped her hands with glee and laughed before running after her grandfather.

*   *   *   *   *

Waiting for you at the altar this fall...

by
Karen Rose Smith

Marriage is meant to be for these sexy single guys...once they stand up as best men for their best friends.

"Just, 'cause I'm having a hard time raising my three little cowpokes does *not* mean I'm looking for a wife!"
—*Cade Gallagher, the hard-nosed, softhearted*
COWBOY AT THE WEDDING (SR #1171 8/96)

"I swear I didn't know she was pregnant when I left town!"
—*Gavin Bradley, the last to know, but still a*
MOST ELIGIBLE DAD (SR #1174 9/96)

"Why is everyone so shocked that I agreed to marry a total stranger?"
—*Nathan Maxwell, the surprising husband-to-be in*
A GROOM AND A PROMISE (SR #1181 10/96)

Three of the closest friends, the finest fathers—
THE BEST MEN to marry! Coming to you only in

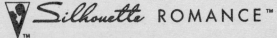 **ROMANCE**™

Look us up on-line at: http://www.romance.net

BESTMEN

MILLION DOLLAR SWEEPSTAKES
AND EXTRA BONUS PRIZE DRAWING

No purchase necessary. To enter the sweepstakes, follow the directions published and complete and mail your Official Entry Form. If your Official Entry Form is missing, or you wish to obtain an additional one (limit: one Official Entry Form per request, one request per outer mailing envelope) send a separate, stamped, self-addressed #10 envelope (4 1/8" x 9 1/2") via first class mail to: Million Dollar Sweepstakes and Extra Bonus Prize Drawing Entry Form, P.O. Box 1867, Buffalo, NY 14269-1867. Request must be received no later than January 15, 1998. For eligibility into the sweepstakes, entries must be received no later than March 31, 1998. No liability is assumed for printing errors, lost, late, non-delivered or misdirected entries. Odds of winning are determined by the number of eligible entries distributed and received.

Sweepstakes open to residents of the U.S. (except Puerto Rico), Canada and Europe who are 18 years of age or older. All applicable laws and regulations apply. Sweepstakes offer void wherever prohibited by law. Values of all prizes are in U.S. currency. This sweepstakes is presented by Torstar Corp., its subsidiaries and affiliates, in conjunction with book, merchandise and/or product offerings. For a copy of the Official Rules governing this sweepstakes, send a self-addressed, stamped envelope (WA residents need not affix return postage) to: MILLION DOLLAR SWEEP-STAKES AND EXTRA BONUS PRIZE DRAWING Rules, P.O. Box 4470, Blair, NE 68009-4470, USA.

SWP-ME96

As seen on TV!
Free Gift Offer

With a Free Gift proof-of-purchase from any Silhouette® book,
you can receive a beautiful cubic zirconia pendant.

This gorgeous marquise-shaped stone is a genuine cubic
zirconia—accented by an 18" gold tone necklace.

(Approximate retail value $19.95)

Send for yours today...
compliments of 🔶 *Silhouette*®

To receive your free gift, a cubic zirconia pendant, send us one original proof-of-purchase, photocopies not accepted, from the back of any Silhouette Romance™, Silhouette Desire®, Silhouette Special Edition®, Silhouette Intimate Moments® or Silhouette Yours Truly™ title available in August, September or October at your favorite retail outlet, together with the Free Gift Certificate, plus a check or money order for $1.65 U.S./$2.15 CAN. (do not send cash) to cover postage and handling, payable to Silhouette Free Gift Offer. We will send you the specified gift. Allow 6 to 8 weeks for delivery. Offer good until October 31, 1996 or while quantities last. Offer valid in the U.S. and Canada only.

Free Gift Certificate

Name: _____

Address: _____

City: _____ State/Province: _____ Zip/Postal Code: _____

Mail this certificate, one proof-of-purchase and a check or money order for postage and handling to: SILHOUETTE FREE GIFT OFFER 1996. In the U.S.: 3010 Walden Avenue, P.O. Box 9077, Buffalo NY 14269-9077. In Canada: P.O. Box 613, Fort Erie, Ontario L2Z 5X3.

FREE GIFT OFFER   084-KMD
ONE PROOF-OF-PURCHASE
To collect your fabulous FREE GIFT, a cubic zirconia pendant, you must include this
original proof-of-purchase for each gift with the properly completed Free Gift Certificate.

084-KMD

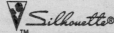

You're About to Become a *Privileged Woman*

Reap the rewards of fabulous free gifts and benefits with proofs-of-purchase from Silhouette and Harlequin books

Pages & Privileges™

It's our way of thanking you for buying our books at your favorite retail stores.

PROOF OF PURCHASE
SR-PP171
Offer expires October 31, 1996

Harlequin and Silhouette— the most privileged readers in the world!

For more information about Harlequin and Silhouette's **PAGES & PRIVILEGES** program call the Pages & Privileges Benefits Desk: 1-503-794-2499

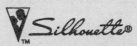

Silhouette®

SR-PP171